D0835314

EXTINGUISHED

EXTINGUISHED

TITANIUM SECURITY SERIES

By Kaylea Cross

ISBN: 978-1494734282
Print Edition

Dedication

I dedicate this book to all those who have served and those
currently serving. And a special shout out to the few and
proud of the United States Marine Corps—Semper Fi.

Author's Note

This is the fourth book of my **Titanium Security** series, and I hope you love Blake and Jordyn's story. I adore friends-to-lovers/best-friend's-little-sister stories, and this one really tugged at my heartstrings. Also, I hope you learn a thing or two about snipers you didn't know before!

Up next is Alex's story. You know how I love older heroes, and this story's gonna be emotionally intense.

Happy reading!
Kaylea Cross

Overview

She's wanted him forever...

For years former Marine Jordyn Bridger has been in love with a man who refused to see her as anything but his best friend's little sister. A mind-blowing kiss finally changed that, but then he disappeared from her life. Now he's back, to recruit her for a job with his NSA-sanctioned Titanium Security team. They're going after the terrorist responsible for the recent attacks on their team and Jordyn is eager to lend her skill set to the hunt. She's determined to prove to Blake that she's capable of holding her own—both in the bedroom and on the battlefield.

He's never walking away again...

Former Marine Scout/Sniper Blake Ellis hid his true feelings for Jordyn for years out of respect for her and her family, but once he learns those feelings aren't one-sided, he can't keep his distance any longer. When a team tragedy thrusts Jordyn into the front line with him on a battlefield, Blake will do whatever it takes to protect her. She's everything he ever wanted in a woman but he was too stubborn to see it. Now it might be too late for them. As they race to capture the terrorist they're hunting, Blake and Jordyn find themselves fighting for their lives. If they want to make it out alive they must work together to defeat an unseen, powerful network that will stop at nothing until their entire team is dead.

This is my rifle. There are many like it, but this one is mine.

My rifle is my best friend. It is my life. I must master it as I must master my life.

My rifle, without me, is useless. Without my rifle, I am useless. I must fire my rifle true. I must shoot straighter than my enemy who is trying to kill me. I must shoot him before he shoots me. I will...

My rifle and I know that what counts in this war is not the rounds we fire, the noise of our burst, nor the smoke we make. We know that it is the hits that count. We will hit...

My rifle is human, even as I, because it is my life. Thus, I will learn it as a brother. I will learn its weaknesses, its strength, its parts, its accessories, its sights and its barrel. I will keep my rifle clean and ready, even as I am clean and ready. We will become part of each other. We will...

Before God, I swear this creed. My rifle and I are the defenders of my country. We are the masters of our enemy. We are the saviors of my life.

So be it, until victory is America's and there is no enemy, but peace!

—*Rifleman's Creed, United States Marine Corps*

PROLOGUE

Seven months ago

The house was quiet. All the guests had finally left. Without Jamie here the house that had been like his second home suddenly seemed so empty.

Blake Ellis entered the kitchen to find Jordyn still putting away the last of the leftover food. She glanced up at him, looking exhausted and tense as she pushed a hand through the tumble of rich brown waves cascading over her shoulder. The sleeveless black dress she wore hugged the lean lines of her body and the black heels accentuated the muscles in her long legs. "Everyone gone now?"

He tore his gaze away from her sexy bare legs and nodded, unsure how to help. "Can I give you a hand in here?"

"No, I'm almost done." She went back to covering the platters of appetizers with plastic wrap and shoved them into the big fridge. "You can go, if you want. You don't need to keep me company."

Yes, I do. He couldn't leave her like this, even though he knew it was probably best if he did. "I'll drive you home when you're ready."

"I can drive myself home."

"You're not driving tonight, Jordyn." He'd stopped after the second round of shots in Jamie's honor a few hours ago. Jordyn had had at least three more since then. And he could tell she was barely hanging on to her control at this point.

Rather than argue, she let out a weary sigh and shut the fridge. "Fine. Thanks."

He nodded.

"Did my parents already go up?"

"About ten minutes ago." Mrs. Bridger had looked like she was on the verge of puking when her husband had rushed her up the stairs and left Blake to see the last of the guests off. The hellish day had taken its toll on all of them.

Jordyn hung up the dish towel, glanced around the spotless kitchen. "Well. Guess I'm done."

Even from where he stood Blake could see the shadows beneath her eyes. Her mother said Jordyn hadn't been sleeping, hadn't been eating since they'd been informed about Jamie's death. "I'll take you home, then."

Jordyn met his gaze. Her deep blue eyes were so full of pent up grief and emotion that Blake worried she might shatter. Throughout the funeral and the reception that followed the graveside service, she'd stayed busy in the kitchen or visiting with the guests.

He knew she'd done it as an escape mechanism and to ease the burden for her parents, especially her mother. But Blake also knew just how badly Jordyn was hurting right now. She'd worshipped her older brother. Blake had too. Jamie's death had ripped open a gaping hole in their lives that would never be filled.

Jordyn followed Blake to the door, pausing to stare at the picture of Jamie her parents had placed on the living room mantel. Him in his dress blues the day of their Marine Corps graduation. Blake had stood in formation next to him on the parade ground.

The early March air held a chilly bite. Blake draped his jacket over Jordyn's shoulders, covering the thin shawl she wore. "Thanks," she murmured with a sad little smile, and it was all he could do not to wrap his arms around her. Instead he led her out to his truck and drove to her place twenty minutes away. In the driveway he hesitated. She seemed so sad and alone, he just couldn't leave her. "Want me to come in for a bit?"

"I'd love some company, if you don't mind." She sounded relieved that he'd asked.

Hell no, he didn't mind. As long as he remembered to keep his hands off her.

He took his shoes off at the door, started a fire in the living room fireplace for her and sat on the couch. She joined him a minute later, leaning her head back against the cushions as she stared at the flames. "That was the hardest thing I've ever had to do," she murmured. "Standing there while they lowered him into the ground."

"Yeah." Blake would never forget the resounding thud of the casket as it hit bottom. Jordyn had visibly flinched.

He turned his head to look at her. The firelight played over her face and reflected off her long brown hair. She looked so lost, so sad, it killed him. She'd held up better than he'd expected during the service. He'd been beside her the entire time but other than gripping his hand tight, she hadn't reached for him. The part of him he kept carefully concealed from her ached for her to reach for him.

She met his gaze, those deep blue eyes glistening with tears. "I miss him," she whispered, her voice cracking.

His heart constricted at the grief on her face. "I know, honey." He lifted a hand to stroke the soft waves of her hair.

A soothing, reassuring gesture, but to him it meant so much more. His muscles knotted with the need to cup her face between his hands and kiss her the way he'd been dying to for so long. He wanted to kiss away the sadness and the grief, replace it with the heat and tenderness burning inside him.

Careful. He knew he was walking a dangerous line. One he couldn't cross. Not now. Not ever.

But something seemed to break inside her at his touch. Her face crumpled. She reached for him. Threw her arms around his shoulders and buried her face into his neck as she began sobbing.

Shit. Blake squeezed his eyes shut and dragged her closer. It was good she was finally letting this out, he told himself. And god-dammit, he fucking loved the way she burrowed so trustingly into his arms.

He locked her to him, trying to absorb some of her pain even as he reveled in the feel of her against him. Soft, warm, needing him. He battled the sharp spike of need he'd kept buried for so long. He held her as she cried herself out, saying nothing, letting the strength of his grip reassure her that she wasn't alone, that he cared.

More than she'd ever realize.

At last she quieted, resting contentedly in his arms. She raised that gorgeous tearstained face to his and met his eyes. He was stunned by the female awareness that shone in her gaze. They stared at each other, the air between them crackling with a sudden sexual tension so thick he could hardly breathe. He gazed down at her, didn't move. He didn't trust himself to—he wanted her too much. Was he misreading this?

But when she slid her hands up to cradle his head, he was done for. He couldn't stop himself from leaning down those few last inches and covering her trembling lips with his.

Jordyn gasped and tightened her hold on his head. Kissed him back with so much hunger it left him reeling.

Heat roared through him. Even as he told himself to go slow, be gentle, the kiss turned wild and molten within the space of a few heartbeats. His tongue was in her mouth, stroking, taking, and she was right there with him. He felt her trembling in his arms, making tiny mewling sounds of pent up need. He wanted to satisfy that need so badly his hands shook. He kissed her hard and deep, tasting a hint of scotch and the salt of her tears on his tongue.

She twisted in his arms and rubbed against his body. Erotic little sounds came from her throat, as if she couldn't get close enough and had been dying to taste him.

Blake was on the verge of losing control and he knew it.

He was seconds away from pushing her flat on her back on that leather sofa and stripping her naked just so he could stroke and taste all that soft, smooth skin. Jordyn. The woman who until a few years ago had been almost like a sister to him.

Before she'd inexplicably become so much more.

Realizing what he was doing—what he was jeopardizing—he broke the kiss. She blinked up at him in confusion, those pretty blue eyes heavy-lidded with desire, pink lips swollen and damp from his mouth.

Fuck.

He tore free of her arms, ignoring the way his body screamed in protest and demanded that he finish what he started. His heart pounded. Jordyn sat frozen on the couch, staring up at him with wide eyes. "Blake, what—"

"No, it's…" *My fault. Fuck.* He dragged a hand over his head, feeling like the worst kind of asshole on the planet. What the hell kind of friend was he? To both her *and* Jamie? His best friend was dead, and he was kissing Jamie's little sister.

He couldn't believe he'd just done something so stupid. She was hurting, lonely, and she'd been drinking. When she'd turned to him for comfort he'd gone ahead and taken advantage of it. Oh, he understood she was more than willing to fuck him right now. But for all the wrong reasons. He had to walk away right now before he lost everything—Jordyn and her parents, as well as Jamie.

"I gotta go," he muttered, already heading for the door.

"Blake!"

Without looking back he shoved on his shoes, walked out the door. He left her staring after him, the memory of that wounded expression on her face eating a hole in his gut. And he couldn't shake the terrible feeling that he'd just ruined the most precious thing in the world to him.

CHAPTER ONE

"Tell me what I need to know and I'll make the pain stop."

The figure in the bed groaned and shifted slightly, the restricted movements telling everyone in the private hospital room he was in a whole hell of a lot of pain. Not that any of them gave a shit.

"Amir. It's not gonna get any better until you give me answers."

Positioned by the door, Blake Ellis leaned back against the wall and watched impatiently as the interrogation proceeded. The air in the room hummed with tension, like a low level electrical charge prickling across his skin.

Alex Rycroft, head of the NSA-sanctioned task force Blake was doing contract work for, leaned over the narrow ICU hospital bed and pinned his silver gaze on the prisoner writhing there. "I've got all day, Amir. And the day after that, too. Think you can take the pain that long?"

Amir finally turned his head toward Alex and opened his eyes. The guy looked like death, but that was to be expected after being shot in the arm two nights ago and opting not to get treatment because he was afraid of capture, then being gut shot and coding on the operating table last night. Hospital staff had removed his respirator about thirty minutes ago, and Alex certainly hadn't wasted any time starting the questioning. Their FBI team member, Jake Evers, stood watch as well, recording everything to be used later on during legal proceedings.

"What…do you…want?" Amir managed weakly.

Alex maintained the aggressive posture, his irritation obvious. Guy might be fifty-one years old, but he was former SF and it showed because he was still intimidating as hell. The urgency was clear. Every hour counted if they were going to get a lead on the terrorist leader behind this latest attack. "I want to know what you were doing in the woods last night."

"You…know."

"I want to hear it from you."

Amir grimaced and closed his eyes, one shaky hand going to the bandages covering his abdomen where the surgeons had stopped him from bleeding out and patched him back up again. His voice was barely audible when he responded. "Trying to kill…woman."

"Who?"

"Zahra Gill." His legs shifted, beads of sweat breaking out on his grayish face.

Alex's expression hardened further, and Blake knew it was because Zahra was sort of like a daughter to him. "Why?"

"Had to," he gasped.

"*Why?*"

Amir shook his head, his face screwed up in an expression of agony. "Please. Give me something."

Blake kept his arms folded across his chest to conceal the way his hands curled into fists. They needed something useful *now*, to prevent whatever attack was coming next. Because from the recent chatter they'd heard, another one was already in the final planning stages. They just didn't know when or where.

"You get nothing until we're done," Alex said coldly. "Why did you have to kill her?"

"Because. Hassani. It was her or me." He turned his face away again, unable to look at any of them.

Glancing across the room, Blake exchanged a look with Hunter Phillips, ex-SEAL and team leader for the Titanium Security crew the NSA had brought on board to help with the investigation. He and Hunter had both been there when Amir had staggered out onto the road from the edge of the forest last night, bleeding to death from the gunshot wound. They'd all known Malik Hassani was behind all this—he'd been targeting their team members for the past few weeks now—but having it confirmed aloud sent a surge of adrenaline through Blake. Judging by Hunter's taut expression, they desperately wanted the same thing.

To get over to Pakistan and cut the head off the snake.

Everyone in the room wanted that. Hell, everyone in the global intelligence community did. Hassani was former Pakistani ISI and had his slimy tentacles in every cog of the machine that powered the country. His latest weapon of choice was a certain Tehrik-i-Taliban Pakistan cell that carried out his dirty work, and both he and his followers were gaining momentum each day he avoided capture.

"He contacted you?" Alex pressed, easing back slightly now that the prisoner was talking.

"No," Amir groaned.

"Then how did you know it was him behind this?"

"My...handler said so."

"Abdullo, the Tajik cell member."

Amir swallowed. "Yes."

"You went with him and the American Army vet you knew as 'Bob' up to Deep Creek Lake to set up the portable EMP device?"

Blake stilled. Nobody knew how the hell Hassani had gotten it, but he'd pulled all kinds of tricks to smuggle it off a US base for the attack. Amir had then used it to knock out power and electronic devices in the area around Deep Creek Lake, where Zahra Gill and Sean Dunphy, another team member, had been staying. The pulse had left them isolated and vulnerable. Blake was glad Zahra had gut-shot the fucker.

"Yes. *Please…*" From the weak rasp in his voice, it was clear Amir was succumbing to pain and exhaustion. Alex risked pushing him beyond the ability to talk if this went on much longer. Blake resisted the urge to check his watch, acutely aware that he had another important meeting to leave for shortly. He shoved the surge of impatience aside, knowing there was nothing he could do to speed this up.

Alex must have seen how worn the prisoner was, because he started firing rapid questions about the other cell members who'd been killed last night. In the dark without the benefit of night vision equipment, Dunphy had still managed to hit both of them. Abdullo had already been dead when Blake and Hunter found him, and "Bob" was unresponsive a few dozen yards away. He'd died before the paramedics arrived.

"You were a hit team, sent in to kill Zahra and the security contractor with her," Alex accused.

Amir shook his head slightly. "No. They…weren't with me then. Insurance from Hassani. In case. Then to…kill me." He broke off and squeezed his eyes shut.

At those words, Alex looked up and met Blake's gaze questioningly. Blake had been the first one to come across the bodies. He considered his response before answering.

What the prisoner said made sense, and they'd suspected it anyhow. From the position of the bodies, it looked like the other two cell members had infiltrated the woods from a different direction than Amir. There'd been no radios of any kind, only cell phones, so it was unlikely there'd been any communication between them during the attack on Zahra and Dunphy. It appeared the other two had been circling around to cut off Zahra, Dunphy, and their fellow cell member Amir from ever reaching the road.

Blake nodded. "The other two were armed with M-4s, and they'd been firing from the northeast, not the west. We found casings spread all over that area, but none where he was." He jerked his chin at the man in the hospital bed. While his buddies had been armed with rifles, Amir had been forced to make do with only a single semi-automatic pistol. Something everyone else in the room was already aware of. Just as they all knew how careful Hassani was.

It made total sense that he'd send in a clean-up squad to ensure Zahra and Dunphy were dead, then kill Amir to guarantee nothing got leaked, and get out with the weapon before anyone realized what had happened. If Zahra and Dunphy hadn't acted so decisively, that's exactly what would have happened.

Alex nodded and brought Hunter in on the questioning next. Blake maintained his place by the door as the session wound to a close. Amir was visibly shaking by the end, the skin of his face stretched taut over the grimace of agony. Only when Alex had received the last bit of intel he was looking for did he relent and look over at Blake with a terse, "Get the nurse."

Amir's audible sigh of relief reached Blake as he left the room and returned with a nurse to administer another hit of morphine from the pump into the IV line. Hunter met him out in the hallway and closed the door behind him.

"That went well."

Blake grunted, anxious to leave the building and get going. "Yeah. Bet he wishes we'd let him die last night though."

"Oh, guaranteed. Asshole's gonna spend the rest of his days rotting in a dark hole surrounded by the enemy. Has a certain sense of poetic justice to it."

Amir's door opened and Evers and Alex filed out. Alex nodded at them and walked over to join them.

"Get what you needed?" Blake asked, fishing his keys from his pocket.

Alex nodded. "For now. I'm just gonna give him a taste of what morphine can do for him before I take it away and go at him again. You guys can head out though. Gage and Claire are working on new intel back at the office," he added, referring to the Titanium team's second-in-command and his NSA analyst fiancée. "Want to grab a bite to eat first?"

Blake ran a hand over his head. "Can't. Gotta see about lining up an interview for Tom." The owner of Titanium Security, who he'd promised this favor.

Hunter eyed him thoughtfully. "Yeah, how come you and Dunphy were all secretive about that yesterday? As co-owner of the company I get to vet all potential employees anyhow, so I'm gonna find out who this mystery person is sooner or later."

Later was just fine with Blake. "No reason." Not one he'd willingly discuss, anyhow.

"How is Dunphy, by the way? Anyone check on him yet?" Alex asked, a wicked gleam in his silver eyes.

"Currently recovering from the worst case of the runs he's ever had," Hunter answered with a grin. Yesterday he'd spiked the prankster's brownies with enough laxatives to turn him into a human prune, and right before Dunphy and Zahra had to get on a plane to Coeur d'Alene to see his family. Good times.

Blake shook his head. "Remind me to never piss you off," he said to Hunter. "You're twice as evil as Dunphy on his best day." Of course, that would only make Dunphy want to up his game when he got back.

Hunter grinned and clapped him on the shoulder. "Don't worry about it—you're not in my line of fire. Yet. Good luck reeling in this mysterious interviewee. Where did you say you were headed?"

"I didn't."

Alex and Hunter both looked at him with intrigued expressions. "There's a definite story there. I wanna know what it is," Alex said to Hunter.

"Me too. It's always the quiet ones who surprise you the most," Hunter said with a shake of his head.

As a former Marine Scout/Sniper, Blake was well trained in the art of evasion. And he definitely knew when to make a tactical withdrawal. "See you guys later."

Before they could ask anything else he turned and strode to the elevator. Right now he faced a long drive into Virginia, followed by a head-on, overdue confrontation with his conscience once he got there.

He was looking forward to it as much as stabbing something sharp into his eye.

The oppressive atmosphere of his temporary quarters was starting to get to him. Forced to stay in three darkened rooms all day and never leaving the place, it felt like the walls were starting to close in on him.

Malik Hassani pushed up from the soft chair in the corner and paced restlessly around the room. It was only his second night at the safe house in Peshawar. He didn't know how many more he'd have. Things were too unsettled for him to leave, even at night with armed guards to protect him. His situation was more precarious now than ever.

Three times now his followers had carried out attacks on the Titanium Security team members who had exposed him, and all of them had failed. By now even those who he'd considered loyal to him in the military and political machine had to be questioning his effectiveness.

But not for long. He'd already set the next plan into motion to ensure he maintained the momentum he'd fought so hard to achieve with his allies. All he needed now was to pull the metaphorical trigger.

At the sound of a car engine approaching the back of the house, Malik withdrew his weapon from the holster on his hip and took up position behind the only door in the room. Away from any of the blind-covered windows. If someone wanted to attack him they'd either have to enter the room or use a bomb.

The front door opened and closed. A familiar voice called out the password for the all clear signal and Malik relaxed slightly. Moments later a knock came at the door to his room.

"Sir?"

"Enter." He kept his finger on the trigger. When the door opened, only his trusted advisor from his ISI days entered and carefully closed the door behind him. Malik motioned Bashir away from the door, his gaze pinned there in case anyone had coerced the man and was waiting in the hall to kill Malik.

"I'm alone."

Malik never took his eyes off the door. He hadn't risen to the status he enjoyed now by being naive or trusting. Something his enemies knew very well. "And?"

"I've personally activated three of the cell members in Washington. They're doing reconnaissance now and the operation is set for Sunday morning."

He nodded and lowered his weapon but maintained some of his focus on the door as he glanced at Bashir. "You're sure they're competent?"

"I'm sure."

His muscles eased. If Bashir felt that confident, it was a good sign. And Malik liked the underscored message of the attack happening on the holiest day of the Christian week. He wasn't a particularly religious man, but he had and would continue to use it as a weapon to further his agenda. "Anything else?"

Bashir wiped a hand over his short beard. "They still don't know where you are. The CIA, NSA and MI6 have traced your calls to the mole in the NSA. Ruth Klassen was arrested yesterday morning."

Ah yes, the woman who'd worked as Alex Rycroft's loyal personal assistant for so many years until Malik had used the lives of her family members in Jordan to garner her cooperation. "And the satellites?"

"As far as we know, none of them have found anything to lead them here. Not yet. But it's still not safe for you to use any electronics."

Because the agencies were still monitoring calls going in and out of Peshawar due to the attempted assassination of American philanthropist Khalia Patterson a few weeks ago. He grunted.

"Another day or so and we'll move you to a safer location. And Amir is still alive."

Satisfied no one was hiding out in the hallway, Malik finally put his weapon away. "He'll talk. Between him and the Klassen woman's phone records they have to know by now that I haven't left Pakistan. They'll be coming after me soon. I know there are already teams in place here." Small squads of men from elite units such as SEAL Team Six or perhaps Delta, who could infiltrate any target and carry out a hit before anyone was even aware of the threat.

But unlike Bin Laden, Malik wouldn't be so stupid as to rely on the loyalty of others to keep him hidden. Except for perhaps Bashir, the only man he truly trusted.

"That's why we'll move you as soon as it's safe." Bashir glanced around the bare, dim room, then settled his gaze on him once more. "Do you need anything?"

He needed to be able to breathe, to finally seize the moment he'd been waiting for and take control of the power he'd earned. "I need the attack in Washington to happen without any problems."

"It will."

Malik nodded, pleased by the man's belief in the team he'd put in place. He didn't care that Bashir's loyalty came partly because he knew he'd hold great power by serving at Malik's side once he seized control. He and Bashir had served in the military together, then gone on to rise through the ranks of the ISI. There was no man on earth he valued more. "Then you may go and get word to the general to be prepared. The Americans will come, and we'll be ready when they do."

CHAPTER TWO

B lake shut the SUV's door and pulled in a deep breath. The damp October air was tinged with the sharp chemical smell of gasoline and motor oil. A light rain pattered his head and shoulders as he made his way to the front entrance of Oorah Custom Rides. His stomach rumbled, hunger mixing with the edge of nerves. Or was it dread? Some of both, he decided as he pulled out his phone. The three hour drive from Baltimore with only a cup of coffee and a donut to sustain him had long since worn off.

He sent off a quick text to his boss, Tom Webster. *Going in. Will report back once I have an answer.*

Against the gray backdrop of the low cloud deck, the garage loomed ahead, its large red steel doors resembling the flat line of a disapproving mouth against the black exterior. Blake steeled himself for what he was about to endure. This meeting should have happened a long time ago and he just wanted to get the awkward part over with.

An electronic doorbell chimed when he opened the front door and stepped inside. A stronger whiff of motor oil hit his nostrils. At the rear of the room a door to one of the shop's bays opened and James Bridger Sr. walked in. The former gunny sergeant's perpetually pissed-off expression dissolved into a wide smile when he saw him standing in the entryway.

"Blake! How the hell are you, son?"

Blake returned the smile and stepped forward to accept the hand offered to him. "Doing well, sir. You?"

"Fine, just fine." He kept a solid grip on Blake's hand, the pleasure on his face doing a decent job of masking the pain Blake could see lurking in those dark eyes. Seeing him couldn't be easy for the man, since it would bring back a lot of memories; some bittersweet, others painful. "You're looking good."

"I'm doing well. You guys seem to be busy here as usual."

Senior released his hand, the fond smile still in place. "It's been steady. Who you working for these days?"

"Fairly new firm called Titanium Security. Run by two former SEALs, good guys."

The man grunted. "They pay you well?"

"I can't complain, sir." Much higher pay was one of the reasons he'd left his beloved Corps for private contract work, and one of the biggest problems cannibalizing the Special Operations Forces ranks across the military.

Senior tilted his head, perusing him with an attentiveness that only those who have served in combat possessed. Even though he was used to the scrutiny, a surge of guilt had Blake fighting the urge to squirm under that penetrating gaze. "You here on a social visit?"

"Wish I was, sir."

"Oh." The smile slipped a notch and Blake felt like a total shit for disappointing him. He'd been like another son to this man for a long damn time. No matter what, Blake should have made more of an effort to put his own shit aside and act like one since the funeral. He hadn't seen anyone in the family since, and now the first time he'd finally found the balls to come here again it was because of business. "You here to see Jordy then?"

It was all he could do to not look away from that intense stare. "Yeah." The old man was weighing him now, and Blake didn't like it because it made him feel like an outsider. Though what did he expect when he hadn't kept in touch in so long?

His gaze slid unerringly to the framed photo on the wall next to the wide desk near the door Senior had come out of. It showed him, Jamie, Senior and Jord dressed up in winter gear, all smiling as they knelt in the forest to hold up the head of an elk buck Jord had tagged two years ago during a hunting trip in the interior of B.C.

He quickly turned his attention back to Senior, the sight of his closest friend in that photo hitting him square in the heart.

The older man nodded once and clapped him on the shoulder. "Go ahead and go on back. Usual place. You'll stay for dinner, right? I'll call Carol and let her know—"

"I'm due back in Baltimore tonight. Thanks for the offer, though." Yeah, he was a total pussy to be making a hit-and-run stop like this. But he'd promised Tom he'd give the invitation in person. Hell, Blake had brought it up in the first place, probably out of some sick and twisted sense of masochism. He'd break the ice, say what he'd come to say and head back to Baltimore.

"You'd better make time to have a beer with me, at least. Been way too long since I've seen you last."

Seven months, to be exact. The day of Jamie's funeral. Blake couldn't refuse this invitation. "That sounds good, sir. Love to." And lord knew, he could use a beer after what was coming next.

"Good." Senior gestured for him to go through to the back with a wave of his hand. "Go say hi and come get me when you're ready to hit the pub."

Blake wasn't here to say hi, but he didn't correct him.

The muted whirr of drills and power socket wrenches hit him full volume the moment he cracked open the door that led to the main auto body shop. Various chassis and car parts lay scattered around the large shop in organized chaos. Several guys glanced up from their work at welding stations or hydraulic hoists then went right back to what they were doing. Blake walked through, noticing the many stations and all the various projects underway.

Propped against the far wall of the expansive building, several car and truck hoods lay waiting to be painted, and a few others were finished and ready to be wrapped up for shipping. Two bore the trademark custom flame motifs he'd recognize anywhere and something tightened in his chest. He passed by them all, heading for the door beside them that would lead to the next warehouse, aware of the rare tingle of nerves deep in his belly.

The moment he pushed open the door to the overflow shop he was assaulted by the hard hitting beat and guitar riffs of Led Zeppelin blasting from a pair of speakers suspended from the ceiling. On the concrete floor beneath the rough body of a hot rod in the initial stages of fabrication, a pair of work boots stuck out from beneath the edge of the frame, the right foot tapping to the rhythm of When the Levee Breaks.

He shut the door behind him, the clang of the door lost in the bone-shaking flood of the music. The boot continued to tap away, a wrench working rhythmically with the beat. Blake stuffed his hands into his pockets and released a deep breath. He was here; might as well just get this part over with so he could get his answer, have that beer with Senior, and head back to the safe house he shared with Hunter and Dunphy.

Berating himself for stalling, annoyed by the lingering anxiety he couldn't seem to shake, he walked over to the large workbench set into the back wall and shut off the stereo. In the sudden silence the boot stopped tapping and a hard sigh emerged from under the vehicle.

The metallic clink of a wrench started up again almost instantly. "Tell Senior not to get his panties in a wad. I'll do the damn hood as soon as I finish with this undercarriage, which he insists has to be shipped first thing in the freaking morning." Annoyance laced every word.

Blake hid a grin. "No, thanks. I don't have a death wish."

The wrench stopped.

Blake withdrew his hands from his pockets to fold his arms across his chest and waited, aware that he was practically holding his breath as Jordyn began to roll out from under the vehicle. Clad in dark blue overalls, those long legs seemed to go on forever as they eased out from beneath the hoist. Long, trim legs that led to strong hips and an ass he had no business staring at, let alone remembering the fantasies he'd had about it.

A slim waist appeared, then the rise of small, firm breasts pushed against the coveralls.

Have mercy.

He mentally groaned, bracing himself for the rest as the face that had haunted him emerged from the shadows. Shocked deep blue eyes fastened on him, the color even more vibrant against her light honey-toned tan and rich brown hair. She'd cropped her hair short, most of it now covered by Jamie's old camo ball cap with the U.S. flag on it.

She pushed her bangs to the side with one grease-stained hand to see him better. Those gorgeous, vivid eyes settled on his with unerring intensity and one dark eyebrow rose in censure. "Well, well, look who it is. To what do I owe the pleasure of being graced with your presence?"

Jordyn considered it a minor miracle that her voice was steady, given that her heart had just done a gigantic somersault and her mouth was completely dry. She hated her body's inevitable reaction to the man, even though she wasn't surprised by it. The sight of him had always hit her hard, right from the first time she'd met him.

"Hey, Jord."

She didn't respond. God, would the sight of this man always hurt? She'd been seventeen when Jamie had brought him home during leave the first year he'd enlisted in the Corps. Back then she'd had a raging crush on him. While to him she'd been nothing more than Jamie's little sister, which, according to the Guy Code Rulebook meant she was sexless and worthy of strictly platonic attention or the occasional brotherly pat on the head.

The memory stung and put her teeth on edge. "Hey yourself." Even after she'd become a Marine, he'd still looked at her as only *Jamie's little sister.* She'd waited years for him to see her as a woman instead of the girl he had to hang with when he visited her family.

Until the night of her brother's funeral and the single scorching kiss that had changed everything. And not in the way she'd always hoped. He'd taken off and she and her parents had barely received an email or phone call from him since.

That pissed her off, but more than that, it *hurt.* Worse than she'd ever admit to him.

He still hadn't said anything else. Getting him to talk was like prying teeth, and this time was no different.

With a sigh she sat up, put her torque wrench down and carefully collected her thoughts before meeting his gaze once more. When she did, she couldn't help but drink in the sight of him, all six feet two inches of hard, buff male dressed in a light gray T-shirt, dark blue jeans and work boots. The material clung to him in all the right places, showing off the effortless power and grace he'd always possessed. The strong planes of his jaw were shadowed with a few days' dark growth.

Set off against his dark caramel skin, those golden hazel eyes stared back at her unflinchingly. Eyes that could scope out a target hundreds of yards away or melt a woman with a single glance.

She'd seen him do both, many times over the years.

Pushing to her feet, she pulled a rag out of her hip pocket and scrubbed at her hands to give herself something to do. It was much easier facing him while standing, when he wasn't towering over her. She was tall for a woman, only three inches shorter than him in her work boots. And she wanted to make it plain that she wasn't the least bit intimidated by this confrontation. "So?" she prompted.

He didn't seem bothered by the sharpness in her tone. "Keeping busy, I see. Saw some of your work in the other warehouse. I can pick out your flames anywhere."

Aww, that was sweet. It still didn't tell her why he was here. "You just stopping by to say hi to my dad?" Her traitorous gaze slid to his broad, muscular chest. Outlined beneath his shirt she could just make out the shape of his HOG's Tooth. The conical hollow point boat round rested right over his heart, marking him as a *Hunter of Gunmen* upon graduating as a Scout/Sniper. Sniper lore said there was ultimately one round destined to end a person's life. If a sniper carried it with him at all times, it could never be fired, making him invincible. Whether or not it was true, it had certainly protected Blake so far.

"No. I'm here about a job."

Covering her surprise, she tucked the rag away and folded her arms across her chest, mimicking his stance. "For me?"

He confirmed it with a nod. "The company I work for is short on security contractors. My boss needs someone with experience and security clearance, and he specifically wants a qualified mechanic as well as someone good with a long gun."

Huh. She definitely qualified, on all fronts. But she was still skeptical. "So you suggested me?"

Another nod. "Dunphy and I both did."

She raised her brows, trying to hide how much it pleased her that he thought enough of her skills to personally recommend her to his boss. Or maybe Dunphy had and Blake was only the messenger. "Dunphy works with you too?"

"We started together a couple months ago."

"So what's the job?" she asked.

"The usual stuff. Stateside and overseas. I promised to come here and deliver a personal invitation to an interview tomorrow in Baltimore. Tom Webster's the owner of Titanium Security. He's only in town until Friday morning, so if you want to think it over you'd better decide pretty quickly."

"Why didn't you just call me instead of driving up here?"

He searched her gaze. "Would you have talked to me?"

"Probably not." Not after he'd kissed her like that then run like a fucking coward.

Something moved in his eyes, but she couldn't say for sure whether it was regret. "That's why."

Jordyn hated the bitterness inside her but she didn't know how to get past it. After pining for him for so long, she'd finally felt his lips on hers, tasted him and run her hands over those delicious muscles in his back and shoulders. One taste, then it had all been snatched away again. "I haven't done contract work for almost nine months." She could sure use the extra pay and the change of scenery though. While she loved her job here at the shop, she was getting bored. And having a chance to use her skill set again in the field? Oh, hell yeah.

"But your security clearance is still valid, right?"

"Yeah." And her shooting was still as good as ever. She and her dad spent hours on the range together firing various weapons to keep their skills sharp. She'd been shooting since she was a kid. "When does your boss need to know by?"

"As soon as possible. Right now would be even better, so I can text him and let him get everything set up."

Now? Not happening. "I'll think about it and let you know."

He didn't seem surprised by her answer, but Blake was a master of hiding his emotions. He had the best damn poker face she'd ever seen. It drove her nuts. "All right. I'm gonna head out for a beer with your dad."

"Don't tell him about the job offer. He won't be too happy about me signing up for an assignment that might put me overseas again." And she could just imagine how her mother would react.

"Sure." His beautiful, gold-flecked eyes swept over her face before he met her gaze again. "It's good to see you again, Jord."

"Thanks. You too," she added grudgingly, even though it was true. She'd been starved for the sight of him. But now that she'd seen him, that old wound had been reopened and all the damn insecurities that came with it rose inside her. Why had he run? Why drop out of her life like that? Did she mean so little to him?

She mentally shook herself. If she was seriously even entertaining the idea of taking this job and maybe working with him at some point on an assignment, then she'd better get past all that baggage in a hurry. He'd clearly moved on. She had to find a way to do the same.

Blake paused, opened his mouth like he wanted to say something else, but then true to his introverted nature, offered a parting smile instead and walked away.

Staring at the back of him as the door closed behind him with a heavy thud, Jordyn dragged a grease-scented hand over her face. What the hell was she supposed to do now? She was already pretty sure she'd take the job if Blake's boss offered it to her. The money would allow her to pay off the rest of her debt and make a sizeable contribution to the nest egg she'd been socking away to buy a house with.

And if the job came with the potential of having to work with Blake in close quarters? She couldn't decide whether that was a blessing or a curse.

✯ ✯ ✯

CHAPTER THREE

"More potatoes, Blake?"

He looked up from his dinner. His plate already held a mound of them, along with a pile of homemade pot roast, his hostess's famous popovers and roasted veggies. "No thanks, Carol."

Jordyn's mom smiled at him and passed the gravy boat. "Well there's lots here, so don't be shy about helping yourself to more if you want it."

"Will do." He still couldn't believe he was sitting here, doing this, after he'd said no to Senior earlier. Blake had been in the bar nursing a beer with him when Carol had called her husband's cell and found out Blake was there. After that, he hadn't had the heart to turn down her excited invitation to dinner. It felt surreal to be seated at the familiar dining room table after all this time. Seeing Jamie's empty spot across from him and knowing his friend would never sit there again put a hard knot in Blake's chest.

"It's like I knew you were coming," Carol continued. "This always was your favorite meal here."

"I loved everything you ever made," he told her.

She beamed at him. "I'm just so happy to have you here again. We've missed you."

And now the knot had a heaping pile of guilt on top of it. "Missed you too." He had, more than they realized. His withdrawal from their family after the funeral had probably confused them as much as it had hurt them. He hated knowing that.

The back door opened and closed. A moment later he caught the faint scent of soap and shampoo as Jordyn entered the room. She stopped in the doorway when she saw him at the table, then quickly averted her gaze and went around the other side to take her place. "I thought you had to be back in Baltimore tonight," she said coolly, not looking at him as she helped herself to some of the roast.

"Yeah, but I couldn't pass up the chance to enjoy your mom's cooking again."

She lifted her eyes to his, the serving fork stuck into a slab of meat. The resentment burning there took him off guard, and suddenly he realized he'd hurt her way worse than he'd realized. He'd expected her to be frosty, but not this angry. "I'm sure she would've packed some up for the road."

Ouch. He hid a wince.

"I asked him to stay, and you missed grace," Carol interrupted, shooting her daughter a narrow-eyed look. Then she turned to Blake with a smile. "So. What's brought you out here today?"

He busied himself with cutting into a popover smothered in gravy. "I had to talk to Jordyn about something."

"Oh?" she looked back and forth between them, but when neither of them said anything more, she focused on Blake again. "What about?"

Senior and Jordyn both got very quiet and kept their eyes on their plates as they ate. Blake set his fork down. He couldn't lie to the woman who'd been like a second mom to him for so many years. Not when he'd already behaved so cowardly. "A job."

Her expression froze, the happiness in her eyes dimming. Averting her gaze, she picked up her water glass. "What kind of job?"

Blake darted a glance at Jordyn, but she wouldn't look at him. He turned back to Carol. "A contracting job with the company I work for."

She focused on her daughter, her shoulders rigid. "Are you thinking of taking it?"

"All he did was offer me an interview," Jordyn answered, forking up a mouthful of potatoes loaded with gravy. He couldn't help but stare at her mouth as her lips wrapped around the fork. "I told him I'd think about it."

Carol turned her gaze back on Blake. "Is it here stateside? Or is it overseas?"

He could see how upset she was becoming, could practically feel the anxiety radiating from her. In that moment, Jamie's ghostly presence seemed to fill the room, the reminder of how he'd died pressing in on them all. Blake still couldn't lie to her. "Probably both." If Jordyn took the job, chances were good they'd get a decent lead on Hassani in the coming days and they'd be on their way to Pakistan.

Carol flashed a forced smile that wobbled around the edges and held up her glass. "Well. I'm glad you're here, at any rate. Now eat up before the gravy gets cold," she finished, her voice rough.

The meal was as delicious as always, and though both Senior and Carol did their best to maintain friendly conversation throughout, they never mentioned Jamie, and Jordyn never said a word to him. He felt her avoidance keenly. Although what did he expect?

After he'd helped clear the table he stood at the sink doing dishes with her. Jordyn's freshly showered scent was delicious and he was far too aware of the trim yet womanly curves in that long, lean body. Her nails were short and neat as always, a hint of grease under them despite her washing up. Not knowing what to say, he stayed silent as he dried and put away the dishes.

When they were done she pulled the drain stopper out and rinsed out the sink. "Tell Tom I'm interested in hearing more about the job," she said, her back to him.

Blake stopped in the act of putting the dinner plates back into the cupboard. He'd never expected her to accept the interview. Hell, part of him had hoped she'd turn it down so he wouldn't be reminded of his guilt every time she walked into the same room. "Okay," he said slowly. "He's probably going to want to do it tomorrow. You free to come into Baltimore?"

"I'll drive in tonight."

"I can drive you in."

"No thanks. I'd prefer having my own car."

Because she'd prefer not to spend any more time with him than absolutely necessary. That bothered him, even though he knew it was his fault. He tried for a diplomatic, practical approach. "You know there's a good chance you'll be assigned to our team if you get the job."

She turned to face him, wiping her hands on a dishrag. Her expression was calm, but her eyes were cool. The only other time he remembered her looking at him like that was when she'd found out he'd proposed to Melissa. "Yeah, so? I can handle it."

He nodded. "I know you can." She was good at what she did, a dead shot with a rifle and professional on the job. This unresolved friction between them had to go though. "But are you sure? I know it's not easy on you, and your mom seemed—"

"My mom will get over it. And I'm a big girl, Blake. All grown up and fully capable of making my own decisions."

The verbal jab hit its mark, making him flinch internally. He was all too fucking aware of just how grown up she was. Had been for a long time. That was half the problem.

"Anyway, if you're so worried about me taking the job, then why did you drive all the way here to offer me the interview?"

"Because I wanted to see you." His answer seemed to surprise her into silence. He fought back a sigh. They had to talk about the night of Jamie's funeral, but he wasn't going to do it here in her parents' kitchen. He owed her an explanation and if they were possibly going to work together they had to put this behind them so it wouldn't get in the way later. "Look, if you're serious about considering the job, then you're tough enough to endure a few hours alone with me. So prove it and drive back with me. I'll bring you home afterward tomorrow."

She stared at him for a second, then lifted her chin. "You sure you're comfortable with that? Because you've done a damn good job of avoiding me since March."

Fuck. He felt like such an asshole for hurting her. He'd missed her like crazy. "I'm sure. We need to talk."

Measuring him with those dark blue eyes, she finally tossed the damp dish towel onto the counter and walked past him. "Fine. Follow me to my place and give me ten minutes to pack."

Jordyn's stomach was a tangled ball of nerves but she refused to let it show.

After so much time apart it was hard to be confined in the front seat of the SUV and not stare at Blake as he drove. She still could hardly believe he'd walked into the shop today. But she was absolutely not going to make a fool of herself a second time and let him know she still loved him—had never stopped. And not a familial *I love you like blood*, although she absolutely did.

No, she was *in* love with him, in the intense and painful unrequited way only a woman who'd fallen for him as a lovesick teenager could. For years she'd hidden her feelings for him, burying them deep in the layers of the camaraderie and trust they'd forged during his friendship with Jamie. Now she was twenty-three to his twenty-nine, plenty old enough for him to finally *see* her. He'd fractured that trust when he'd all but cut contact since Jamie's funeral. And still her heart wouldn't let go of him.

"So, your mom's good? And John?" she asked a minute after they'd left her place because she had to say something to alleviate the palpable tension between them. Blake had the radio on low and the wiper blades swished every few seconds to clear the light rain falling.

"Both doing great. They travel quite a bit, and every couple of months they go back to Louisiana to see my sisters and their kids. They're real hands-on grandparents."

"I bet. And knowing your mother, she's no doubt impatient for you to get married and give her more grandkids."

"Pretty much, yeah," he said with a fond smile.

God, the thought of him settling down and having a family with someone else put a crushing weight on her chest. His parents were wonderful people and their family was as tight as hers despite their geographical separation. Their lives could easily have been much different. After his biological father had taken off when Blake was just a baby, his mom had raised him on her own until Blake was five and she'd met John. They'd gotten married soon after and had two daughters together, yet John had never treated Blake as anything but his own son. Jordyn respected the hell out of the man for that.

"Do you see them often?" she asked.

"Not often enough. I've been all over the place working contract jobs."

That was the excuse he'd chosen to explain why he'd practically disappeared from everyone's lives for more than half a year. The small talk was grating on her nerves though and they couldn't keep dancing around the real issue at hand. She pushed out a long breath. "So, let's just do this. About that night," she began.

It was subtle, but she didn't miss the slight tightening of his expression and the way his grip shifted on the steering wheel. Still, he nodded. "Yeah, about that."

She waited, telling herself to calm down and not panic about the pause that followed. Whatever he was going to say, it had to be said. She'd just have to suck it up like the big girl she'd told him she was. Only she was fucking terrified that her heart might stop beating if he told her that kiss had been a mistake.

"I'm sorry."

That was it. Two words. Jordyn swallowed and held her tongue, praying he wasn't apologizing for kissing her.

He shot her a sideways glance, sighed when she didn't respond. "I shouldn't have done it."

Oh, shit. Her stomach plummeted like an anvil. Reeling from the impact, not knowing how she was going to handle it, she didn't say a word.

"We were both emotional that night and I shouldn't have touched you like that. I wasn't thinking straight. I felt like such a shit afterward and then I didn't know what to do to fix it, so I thought it was best if I...left."

My God, he not only regretted kissing her, it had made him feel like shit for doing it. She took a deep breath, willed her heart to keep beating as the tiny, stubborn flame of hope burning there was brutally snuffed out. The pain was far worse than she'd thought it would be, considering she'd been bracing for this. It felt like she was bleeding on the inside. "Okay," she answered slowly, surprised her voice was working. "Why?"

He frowned. "Why what?"

"Why would it make you feel like shit?" Hadn't it been obvious that she'd wanted him to kiss her? That she'd been dying for it and had been for *years*?

"Uh, because it was *wrong* of me," he said, as if it was the most obvious thing in the world and he couldn't understand why she didn't see it too. "I crossed the line and it wrecked our friendship. I'm sorry for that. I want to fix it, get back to the way we used to be."

Back to when she was just Jamie's little sister to him, he meant.

The realization made her throat ache with grief. She quickly looked away from him, afraid he'd see the devastation in her eyes. Shock and disbelief slid through her, numbing and cold. She'd been in love with him for so long and he'd never realized it, not even after that kiss or the e-mails she'd sent him. How could he not have known? Or had he just not wanted to? Worse, he felt nothing for her aside from affection and friendship. How was she supposed to deal with that?

"Hey, you gonna say anything?" he prompted with a nervous laugh, glancing over at her. "I'm kinda out on a limb here all by myself."

Out on a limb was better than having your heart smashed to pieces by the person you loved. "What do you want me to say?" she managed, her voice hoarse. Driving with him was a mistake. Now she had to endure the rest of the trip while trying to smother her grief.

"Just say you forgive me and that we can fix it. I already lost Jamie. I don't want to lose you too." His tone was quiet and sincere, and she knew as a man of few words that the admission hadn't been easy for him.

But I can't be just your friend, she wanted to shout at him, battling the pressure of tears at the back of her throat. She couldn't just turn her feelings on and off like a fucking faucet, even for him. "I just—I need some time," she made herself say. Time to recover from this blow, and more time to let the idea of him go. God, how did she even go about that? She wasn't sure if she could ever go back to the way things used to be. There was no way she could hide all the longing and hurt inside her forever, and she shouldn't have to.

He looked away from her, focusing back on the road as he merged onto the freeway that would take them to Maryland. His mouth thinned. "Okay. I understand."

No, you fucking don't understand.

She turned her head to stare blindly out her window and blinked fast, locking everything inside until she was alone later. God, she would not cry in front of him. That would be the ultimate humiliation on top of everything else. Why the hell had she agreed to such a long drive with him? Just because he'd thrown down the equivalent of a dare and she hadn't been able to let it slide? She'd always been too impetuous.

"I really am sorry, Jord."

Yeah, she got that. Far too fucking well. She forced a nod.

He reached over and nudged her thigh with his hand, oblivious to her internal suffering. "You don't hate me, right?"

She swallowed again. "No, I don't hate you." She could never hate him.

Although it would be a hell of a lot easier for her to move on if she could.

CHAPTER FOUR

When Blake made the final turn onto the quiet residential street leading to the safe house he shared with Hunter and Dunphy, he had to hold back a sigh of relief. His apology, lame though it was, hadn't gone over nearly as well as he'd hoped.

In between little stretches of conversation about the job Tom had in mind, Jordyn had been uncharacteristically quiet and withdrawn, and that had made for a long-ass drive back to Baltimore. He hated feeling off center with her, when they'd always been so comfortable with each other in the past. He was at a complete loss as to how to make it better.

You are such *a shit!*

"Wait, I thought you were going to drop me off at hotel?" Jordyn said.

"You're not staying at a hotel, Jord." Not when his safe house was a much more secure location for her. "There've been a few security concerns with the team lately, so to play it safe for the time being you're better off here with me and our team leader, Hunter." He wanted her near him, just in case.

She eyed him, half turning in her seat. "What kind of security concerns?"

"Can't tell you most of it, but I'm sure you've seen the news lately." She was smart enough to piece the rest together.

Her eyes widened. "You mean the bombing at the house in Baltimore a week or so ago? Was that one of your guys who was injured?"

"Gage, our 2IC. And he's fine." And Blake wasn't going to mention the recent attack on Zahra and Dunphy, either. Once again his conscience was needling him about bringing her into what could be a dangerous situation. Yeah, she was good and yeah, she would be an asset to the team. Could he live with himself if she got the job and her life was endangered because of it? Because he'd suggested her in the first place? The closer they'd come to the safe house, the stronger that worry had become. However fucked up they were, he had damn intense feelings for Jordyn and he would die before he let anything happen to her.

"Were you there when it happened?" Concern laced her every word.

"Yeah, but we've all been moved to new locations just in case. Tom or Hunt will brief you fully if he hires you. For now, you're staying with me." He'd sleep easier knowing she was under the same roof as him. While she was here, he was going to make damn sure he watched out for her. If she was offered the job and took it...he'd deal with the rest then.

"Nice of you to mention this now that we're here," she muttered wryly. "I only brought one weapon with me."

He shot her a pointed, sideways glance. Did she seriously think he'd let anything happen to her? "If you're with me, you won't need one."

"Okay, true enough," she said with a little smile. "But you know I can take care of myself."

Ordinarily he'd agree wholeheartedly with that, since he'd seen her handle weapons more times than he could count and knew she was a deadly shot. But she had no idea about the kind of threats they faced from the TTP cell Hassani was using as his personal hit squad, and that weighed heavy on him. Though he wanted to tell her everything, he couldn't.

If Tom hadn't assured him the job he wanted to offer Jordyn was strictly as support and maintenance, Blake would never have agreed to recruit her. Being attached to the team in any capacity was dangerous enough. He felt responsible for her safety, and not just because of his ties to her family.

"Why'd you recommend me to Tom for this job, anyway?" she asked as he pulled into the driveway of the two-story beige stucco house.

"He wanted someone in the area, someone we trusted and could work with, one with your qualifications and service record." She was the first person he'd thought of.

She looked away to stare out her window as he killed the engine. "I'm glad you trust me that much."

He frowned. What the hell was that supposed to mean? Of course he trusted her. "Come on. Let's get you squared away."

He found Hunter at the kitchen table working on his laptop. Hunt stood when he saw Jordyn, and Blake caught the flash of surprise on the man's hard face. "This is Jordyn Bridger. She's interviewing with Tom in the morning. Jordyn, Hunter Phillips, our team leader."

Hunter stuck out his hand and shook Jordyn's. "Nice to meet you."

"You too," she answered, withdrawing her hand to run her fingers through her short cap of hair. "Sorry about just showing up here like this. Blake kind of sprung that on me at the last second."

"No problem." Hunter turned his light brown gaze on Blake, clear amusement there. "Okay, now I get it."

"Get what?" Jordyn asked with a frown, glancing back and forth between them.

"Nothing," Blake answered, and grabbed her duffel. "You can take my room upstairs." He turned and walked out of the kitchen before either of them could say anything else.

With every step he was aware of Jordyn behind him. As he turned to hit the stairs, the fresh clean scent of whatever it was she used on her hair and skin teased his nostrils. In his room he set her bag down on the queen size bed and turned to face her. "Connecting bathroom's through there," he said lamely as he pointed, aware that she could see that for herself.

She stood in the doorway taking in the room and for some reason the space between them grew thick with tension. Given the opportunity to stare at her while her gaze was focused elsewhere, he couldn't help himself. With her profile to him he could see the sweep of her long, thick lashes and the strong line of her jaw. The thin black sweater she wore hugged the small but enticing curves of her breasts and those snug jeans made her legs look a mile long. Legs he'd imagined wrapped around his back or shoulders way too often in his fantasies.

She turned those frank, deep blue eyes on him and he felt the impact ricochet in his chest. "So where are you sleeping?"

Unbidden, an image of them tangled together naked in his sheets popped into his head. He blocked it with ruthless control and shoved the picture back into the forbidden box it had come from. "Dunphy's room. He won't be back until Sunday night."

"I can take his room."

"Naw, it's fine." The truth was, he liked the idea of her in his bed. Something primal in him wanted her there, surrounded by his scent on the sheets. She was still far too distant and he couldn't shake the fear that he'd permanently ruined things.

He was searching for something to say, something that would begin healing the damage he'd done to their relationship, when his cell buzzed in the back pocket of his jeans. Pulling it out, he saw the text from Tom. "Your interview's at oh-seven-hundred tomorrow." His boss seemed pretty eager to interview her. Blake didn't blame him—Jordyn had one hell of a resume.

"Sure, that's fine."

He typed back a response to Tom, then put the phone away and stuck his hands in his back pockets. Jordyn hadn't moved from the doorway, as if she didn't want to get too close to him. Seeing her there, so close but too far away to touch only reminded him of that crazy, white-hot kiss they'd shared. He remembered it vividly, every last detail.

But the fact was, he couldn't have taken things further that night, not without losing her. The irony was, it looked like he'd lost her anyway.

"Need anything?" he made himself ask. Did she think about that night all the time too? Wish it had ended with him deep inside her, then waking up the next morning with his arms around her?

She shook her head. "No, I'm all set. Thanks."

He'd give her some space then. "Okay. Sleep well. I'll drive you to the interview in the morning."

"All right. G'night."

"G'night." He stepped out into the hallway and shut the door behind him.

They just needed time, he decided, remembering her earlier words to him. Once they adjusted to being around each other again, things would go back to normal. Hoping that was true, he headed downstairs. When he came back into the kitchen, Hunter was still working on the laptop. "Anything important come up while I was gone today?"

"Just some more surveillance on a couple more suspected cell members. Evers and I did some recon this afternoon. Alex has been busy dealing with the Amir situation. Guy's given up what little he knows already. Doubt we'll get anything more useful out of him." Hunter sat back and stretched his arms above his head before folding them across his chest and regarding him with keen eyes. "So. About Jordyn. Anything I need to know?"

He'd known this was coming. "I've known her family a long time. Her brother and I served together, we were really close. He died seven months ago on an anti-piracy contract job in Somalia."

"Sorry."

Blake nodded. Missing a fallen buddy never went away; it was only the ache that dulled over time. "Jordyn's good. Almost as good with a rifle as me, and way better with mechanics than anyone I know. Most of her family's served with the Corps and her dad was a gunny sergeant stationed out at Pendleton for more than a decade. He was tough on her growing up, expected the same discipline from her as her brother. She's solid and a hard worker with a good skill set."

Hunter absorbed all that with a single nod. "And in a tight spot, would you want her guarding your back?"

"Absolutely." He said it without hesitation and Hunter nodded again.

A small smile. "Can't wait to find out more about her."

"She's a real team player. You'll like her." It would be hard not to. Jordyn was easily the most interesting person he'd ever known, as well as one of the most talented. Not many women could take down a bull elk with one shot at five hundred yards or build a custom hotrod from the wheels up, let alone hold their own with a bunch of hard-headed, foul-mouthed Marines.

Fewer still could earn their male counterparts' admiration while managing to hold onto that indefinable female essence that made every man in the room aware of her on a primal level. Jordyn had all of that and more. People could depend on her and she was easy to be around.

Except apparently for him, since he'd spent way too much time over the past seven months fantasizing about what her naked body would feel like beneath his if he'd let things go further between them that night. And that made him *such* a skeezy asshole.

He pulled a chair out from the table and scooted in next to Hunter. "Okay, show me what I missed." Maybe that would distract him from the thought of Jordyn curled up in his bed upstairs.

Blake was waiting for her when Jordyn emerged from the second floor conference room at NSA headquarters at Fort Meade the next morning. He rose from the bench he'd been sitting on and tucked his phone away as he offered her a smile. She struggled to ignore her body's inevitable reaction to the sight of him as he spoke. "How'd it go?"

"Good, I think. Man, that was a lot of paperwork I had to fill out though. I'd forgotten how intense this all is." She had a solid feel for the company and the men behind it at least. Tom—a former SEAL in his late forties—and Hunter had both asked her questions, then Alex Rycroft had joined them for a few minutes. "Alex is running the last bit of my background check right now, and Tom and Hunter are checking one more of my references."

Although she couldn't be certain, for things to be moving so quickly they must have done the bulk of the screening prior to the interview. Her gut told her the job was hers. Question was, did she truly want this? Yeah, the money was great and the change of scenery would be nice. But mostly she wanted to make a difference again and put her skill set to good use. If she could be an asset to Blake and the others, she wanted to do it.

"Guess they liked what they saw," Blake said, the golden flecks in his eyes standing out as he smiled. The night he'd kissed her, they'd been molten with desire. She pushed the thought aside.

Not wanting to seem overly confident, she shrugged. "So, now what?" She looked away from the tempting sight of male perfection before her to scan the hallway they stood in.

"We could grab something to eat before I take you back to the house."

"Sure." She fell in step beside him as they headed for the elevators at the end of the hall.

In the cafeteria they sat together at a table in the corner, sipping coffee and snacking on muffins while they both fumbled for things to say to fill the silence. Jordyn tried her best to loosen up, but something inside wouldn't let her. So ironic that she'd finally ended up in Blake's bed, just not the way she'd always envisioned it. After he'd left his room, sleep had been a long time coming and once it did it had hit her hard. She'd been practically unconscious when her phone's alarm had woken her at five-thirty.

She'd just popped the last bite of muffin into her mouth when Blake's cell chimed. He pulled it out, read whatever was on the screen and a sardonic smile spread across his lips. Those golden hazel eyes flicked up to hers. "That was fast."

"What was?"

"Wait for it."

Before she could ask him what the hell that was supposed to mean, her phone rang. She'd only received it back from security a few minutes before the interview ended because they'd had to check it. She dug it out of her pocket and blinked when she saw an unknown caller's number. "Hello?"

"It's Tom. We checked your references and security clearance and everything looks good. You want the job?"

Holy hell, they worked fast. "Yes, I do."

"Then you're hired. Have Blake bring you up to Alex's office to sign the paperwork. You'll be attached to my crew through the NSA taskforce."

She met Blake's amused gaze. "Now?"

"Now," Tom confirmed. "See you upstairs."

She hung up, feeling a little disoriented. "Wow, okay. Guess they're desperate for a mechanic, huh?"

"Ready to head upstairs?" He rose and grabbed the empty cups and wrappers, tossed them in a nearby trashcan.

"Yeah."

On the floor where Alex's office was, she stepped out of the elevator and followed Blake past an empty desk. It seemed weird to have such a prominent workspace empty. Shouldn't someone have been there to direct people once they got off the elevator?

"Ruth's gone."

She half turned to him. "Ruth?"

"Alex's prior assistant," Blake told her as they passed by.

"Oh." Had she died or something?

"Long story," he said quietly, "but the short answer is that she's under arrest. I'm sure Alex will fill you in once you sign the contract."

The one procuring her confidentiality along with the terms of employment. "Okay."

But Alex wasn't in his office. A young woman stood there instead, and smiled at them when they entered. "Hi, I'm Corinne, from the legal department. Alex is in another meeting but he asked me to review this with you."

Blake gestured to the door. "Want me to leave?" he asked her.

"No, you can stay." Jordyn sat in the chair offered to her and went through the contract with the woman. Since it all looked good on her end, she read it over again and signed all three copies.

Corinne put out her hand. "Welcome aboard."

Jordyn shook it, a surreal feeling overtaking her. Alex and Tom sure knew how to cut through red tape. Rising from her chair, she took her copy of the agreement and looked at Blake. "So...now what?"

"Let's go down the hall and I'll introduce you to the rest of the team."

At the very end of it was a big, sleek conference room. Blake opened the glass door for her. Four people looked up as she entered, two men and two women. She broke into an easy grin when she saw Sean Dunphy at the table, working on a laptop next to a pretty dusky-skinned woman with long black hair.

"Jord, how the hell are you, hon?" he asked, jumping up from his chair to stride over and envelop her in a bear hug.

"I'm great. It's good to see you," she said as she pulled back. He still had that devilish gleam in his eyes.

"This is Zahra, translator and hacker extraordinaire," Sean said, indicating the woman he'd been sitting beside.

The look in his eyes when he gazed at the woman told Jordyn all she needed to know. Not once in all the time she'd known him had Dunphy ever looked at a woman like that. He was into her, deep, and it was sort of unreal and awesome to see. "Hi."

Zahra's welcoming smile turned into a grimace as she got to her feet and Sean rushed over to help her out of her chair. That's when Jordyn noticed the bandages around her left calf. "Sorry, I'm not usually so slow," Zahra said and shook Jordyn's hand. "Still recuperating."

"No worries." Jordyn cast a glance at Sean and then Blake for a clue as to what that meant, making a mental note to ask Blake later. Clearly something had happened to her that no one wanted to talk about.

Before she could say anything more, Blake spoke. "Everyone, this is Jordyn Bridger, the newest member of our team." Zahra and the two people she hadn't been introduced to yet stared at her and Jordyn forced a smile. "That's Gage," Blake told her, indicating the tall, well-built man on the other side of the table. He was somewhere in his early forties with short red-gold hair and bright blue eyes. Both arms were covered in full sleeves of tats. His whole demeanor screamed military authority.

"Hey, nice to meet you," Gage said in a deep voice tinged with a southern drawl, and reached out a big hand to shake hers. The tats stopped right at the end of his wrist.

Jordyn shook his big hand. "You too."

Next Blake indicated the woman beside the second-in-command, somewhere around thirty with shoulder length caramel brown hair and pretty gray eyes. "This is Claire, one of our techno wizards. And Gage's better half."

"I can't argue with that." Gage grinned as Jordyn and Claire shook hands.

She could still feel that intense blue gaze on her as she pulled her hand free of Claire's. She couldn't help but glance at Gage.

He was eyeing her thoughtfully. "So, you're her."

"Sorry?"

"I'm looking forward to seeing you put some rounds downrange," was all he said.

"Oh. Sure, whenever you want." Wasn't some kind of test, since she'd already been hired. But so far it looked to her like she was the only female here with military training. She was used to that though, and had no problem with proving herself to her male counterpoints. Once they saw her with a rifle, they usually stopped resenting having her around. She hoped that was true for these guys. Not that she'd have much opportunity to prove herself in a support and maintenance role.

"So, Jordyn," Gage continued as he dropped back into his chair and maintained eye contact. "How much do you know about our team?"

"Not much."

"Then let's bring you up to speed."

She sat and pulled her chair into the table as Blake took the seat next to her. The man smelled delicious, soap and clean male musk. Doing her best to ignore the distraction he posed, she focused on what Gage was saying about the current security situation.

Two minutes in, a flurry of activity broke out in the hall-way. Gage trailed off with a frown and peered through the glass door as the others swiveled in their chairs to see what was going on. Seconds later Alex appeared on the other side of the door. He thrust it open and strode in, his face grim. Hunter was right behind him, his expression scary to behold. Jordyn's hands curled around the armrests in reflex.

While Hunter stayed off to the side of the room, Alex picked up a slim remote from a table on the far side and pointed it at a TV screen mounted on the wall. "Take a look at this."

The screen flashed on to show a female news reporter standing in front of a burning building, and the caption at the bottom read Breaking News. Alex turned up the volume just in time to catch what she was saying.

"Sources now say that a third explosion has gone off a little under ten minutes ago, this one at another residence in a Baltimore suburb. Police say they are searching for the bombers. From eyewitness accounts, possibly as many as seven men are involved in this latest attack to rock the city."

Beside her, Blake tensed. Jordyn looked away from him to glance around the table, and every single person's eyes were glued to the screen as the picture flashed from the burning house to a different building.

The reporter continued. "Officials have not yet confirmed the number, but there are reports that four people were killed in this blast alone, and many more were injured." The footage showed images of what looked like an apartment building fire. People stood out on the sidewalk across the street, staring at the flames while fire crews rushed to douse the blaze. Young children were crying, clinging to their parents. Zahra had a hand over her mouth. Jordyn's skin prickled.

"That's my old apartment building," Zahra said shakily. Sean slid his arm around her shoulders and bent to murmur something in her ear.

"And the first one was my place," Alex added tightly, the muscles in his jaw flexing as he stared at the screen.

Jordyn sucked in a breath. What the hell? Under the table, she reached out and sought Blake's hand. He wrapped his fingers around hers and squeezed once in reassurance but didn't let go and she was glad. Targeted attacks on the team members' previous residences?

While everyone absorbed that new information, Alex reduced the volume and turned to face them all. "Three coordinated bombings on three separate targets in the past hour—my old place, Zahra's, and another NSA safe house no one was supposed to know about. They either found the locations from Ruth before we arrested her, or they have better intel than we thought they did, because they planned this strike carefully. It's Sunday, which speaks volumes in itself, but this attack was carefully synchronized."

His silver gaze swept around the room, resting on each one of them, and Jordyn felt a shiver of unease zip up her spine. "Hassani wants us to know how close he is. He failed to get us twice before, but he's letting us know he's only one step behind." He tossed the remote onto the conference table with a clunk, anger and frustration pulsing off him in waves. "Everybody break into teams and get ready to go wheels up. We're gonna go nail this bastard."

CHAPTER FIVE

"I just heard from Jalil. All three targets have been destroyed."

Malik leaned back in the comfortable leather chair he'd been reading in and regarded Bashir thoughtfully. Having both grown up poor, risen through the ranks of the military and then through the ISI together, they understood each other in a way no one else could. They also both hated how weak the current government's foreign policies were. "Excellent." It was the first good news he'd had in a long time. "Casualties?"

"A few. One of the cell members was injured in the second blast. His wounds weren't life threatening but they're severe enough that he'll need treatment. The authorities will be questioning him within a few hours, I think."

Malik waved that concern away. "No matter, Amir will have told them the same information already. It's time for us to move on."

Bashir's gaze sharpened. "To where? Karachi?"

"No. I plan to stay local for a while longer."

He frowned. "I think that's unwise, considering the amount of pressure they'll be putting on our network to locate you. I'd feel better if we moved you to a different city, at least for a day or two."

"No. I'll stay here until I'm ready to use my escape route. Traveling anywhere else now would be stupid. I'll be crossing the border soon enough." And then he'd escape into the mountains and accept the hospitality of the Taliban leaders he'd so carefully garnered over the years.

Bashir sighed, resigned to following orders. "When?"

"When I decide I'm ready," he said in a hard tone, resenting that his plan was being questioned. "They'll be coming here now. I want them on our soil before I make my next move." The NSA's Alex Rycroft would be here soon. It wouldn't do to escape the Americans unnoticed.

For his plan to work, he had to wait for the chase to begin in earnest. Then he'd draw them into his carefully laid trap. The rugged mountain terrain to the west was treacherous for enemy forces at the best of times. Malik was going to ensure the people coming after him would never make it out alive.

"Get me a secure line," he commanded. "I need to make some calls." Intelligence agencies would be monitoring transmissions in the area but he had to take the risk of exposure in order to capitalize on the protection he'd garnered from certain members within the military, ISI and Taliban groups over the past few years. It was time to call in the favors owed to him.

"Yes, sir."

Malik stood and stretched his back before crossing to the small desk on the opposite side of the room and gathering the paperwork he'd set there. The files included names, contact information and various goodies that he could use to blackmail the men if they suddenly had a change of heart and tried to renege on their promises to him. He had it all on an external thumb drive he kept on a chain around his neck, but using a computer here to review the material would have been stupid. Before he left this location he'd make sure the paperwork was destroyed.

He spoke to Bashir without looking at him. "Have the bodyguards bring the car for me as soon as it gets dark. I want to sleep in that next safe house tonight." It would likely be the last good sleep he got for the next few days at least, but the end result would be worth it.

Seated between Sean Dunphy and Evers as the Air Force C-130 lifted off the runway at Landstuhl in Germany, Jordyn took a deep breath and let it out slowly to dispel the tension inside her. Things had been tense after Alex's announcement back in the NSA conference room, and she felt like she'd been caught up in a whirlwind ever since.

This flight had been the first one available to Qatar, which was why Alex had gotten them all on board. From there they'd hop another flight to Islamabad. Now all ten of them—including Tom and Evers—were crammed into jump seats on either side of the plane's cargo area, which was filled with pallets of supplies and two armored vehicles destined for military personnel stationed at Bagram in Afghanistan.

Next to her, Sean had his head back against the bulkhead, his right arm draped possessively across Zahra's shoulders as she snuggled into him and tried to sleep. They were all tired and trying to nap when they could but Jordyn was too keyed up to sleep at the moment.

She now knew the bandage on Zahra's leg was from a bullet wound sustained the previous weekend during a run-in with a TTP cell member sent to hunt her at Malik Hassani's command. During the flight to Germany, she'd also found out from Gage about Sean's unfortunate—albeit likely well-deserved—predicament that had followed.

Knowing he wasn't sleeping yet, she leaned toward him to be heard above the noise of the four turboprop engines and spoke close to his ear. "So, I hear you had an unfortunate encounter with some laxative-laced brownies."

He cracked one deep brown eye open at her and smirked. "Yeah. It was the shits."

Laughing, she shook her head. "Only you, Dunphy."

"I know," he said with a nostalgic sigh. "They got me good. Kind of awesome, actually."

He *would* think so. "Does Zahra know what she's in for with you?" The analyst seemed pretty straight-laced, but maybe that's what made it work; her seriousness balancing Sean's mischievous side.

"Yep, and she's good with it. Of course, with her I'll just pull harmless little pranks. I save my A game for these guys." He indicated the teammates seated on the other side of the cargo area with a jerk of his chin.

Yeah, she could only imagine what lay in store for the male team members once they set up shop in Pakistan. "Even that laxative revenge didn't teach you anything, huh?"

"Course it did. Taught me next time I've gotta bring out the big guns." He said it with such relish that she couldn't help but grin. She'd bet he already had something planned out and ready to execute when the time was right. Although from the stories she'd heard about him from her brother and Blake over the years, Sean wasn't exactly known for his sense of timing. At least when he was in operational mode he dropped the clown act.

On her other side, Jake Evers tapped her politely on the arm. "You hungry?" He held up the open bag of chips he'd pulled out of the duffel at his feet a few minutes ago.

"Thanks." They'd snagged a sandwich at the base but she was far from full. She took a handful and started to munch, perusing the rest of the team seated across the belly of the cargo area of the plane. Talk about a learning curve. She understood why Blake hadn't told her about all the recent attacks on the team, but it was still a lot to take in. Hard to believe she was now in the middle of it.

"Bet you haven't traveled in style like this for a while," Evers remarked.

"Not for a while, no. Can't say I've missed it." Although she did miss the Corps sometimes. It had challenged her, forced her to dig deep and forged her into a stronger, more confident person. She'd served four years before applying for and receiving an honorable discharge. Her memories of her service were some of the best and worst at the same time.

"Well, at least your quarters will be better than anything you stayed in with the Corps."

The jump seats were gonna make for one hell of a long, uncomfortable ride to Qatar, that's all she knew. "I'm pretty stoked about that. Alex said there might even be the possibility of hot showers in our future." That would be a welcome change. Marines had notoriously shitty luck when it came to accommodations, rations and equipment, and often had to make do with whatever was leftover once the Army and Air Force were outfitted.

Evers grinned, showing off even white teeth, his brown eyes twinkling. "Only the best for us. You seem to be settling in pretty well so far. I know there's been a lot to take in."

She didn't know too many Feds, but she liked Evers already. And he wasn't hard on the eyes, with his dark good looks and broad shoulders. He'd done eight years in the Army and finished as a captain. "You could say that, yeah. Looks like we've got a good mix of people on the team though."

Claire and all the remaining guys on the team were sprawled in the seats on the opposite side of the aircraft, arms crossed, chins resting on their chests as they tried to snatch some Zs. By now Jordyn had a pretty good feel for their personalities.

Hunter was the grim, serious one, the undisputed leader, and the most intimidating of the group. Gage was the friendly one of the group but he had a hard edge to him that came with being in command of men for so many years, and she had no trouble at all picturing him in the position of Team Daddy he'd served as for so many years with Special Forces. Sean of course was the prankster, although he was a gifted spotter and a total pro when he was working. And then there was the quiet, professional man that captured her attention without even trying.

Jordyn let her gaze slide to Blake, and was startled to find him staring back at her. His normally taciturn expression was gone, replaced by a slight frown between his brows and his delectably full lips were thinned as if he was annoyed. Then his eyes flicked to Evers and a rush of understanding hit her.

He thought she was flirting with Evers? He obviously didn't like it. Or maybe he thought Evers was flirting with her, she wasn't sure, but seriously? It pissed her off, since he had to know her better than that. Yeah, Evers was hot and seemed like a nice guy. That didn't mean she'd openly flirt with a member of the team she'd just been assigned to.

Sending Blake an icy glare, she turned her attention back to Evers, who was much more pleasant company and didn't make her stomach knot into a ball every time she looked at him.

He also didn't create any butterflies in there either.

She settled into an amiable conversation with him and tried to force Blake from her mind. It didn't work. He'd been giving her the distance she'd asked for, yet somehow that hurt worse. She was more conscious of him than ever, right there on the other side of the plane. It made her chest ache to leave things between them this way. They wouldn't see each other much once they arrived in Pakistan. As soon as they got settled into their quarters she'd have to set things right between them before he headed out. If anything happened to him out there she'd never forgive herself for not mending the rift between them.

Nodding at something Evers was saying, she snuck another glance back at Blake. As though he felt her gaze on him his eyes opened and locked on hers. He held her stare for a few seconds, his expression unreadable, then broke it by closing his eyes and settling into a more comfortable position to sleep. She couldn't help but notice those muscular arms folded across his wide chest, or the way her heart rate increased at the sight of him. Even though she got that he didn't have romantic feelings for her, she knew he still cared and that was the hell of it. She was starting to think she'd never be able to fall out of love with him completely, and her naughty side still demanded that she lick every inch of that caramel-toned skin.

Tearing her gaze away from him, she looked back at Evers and realized he was waiting for an answer. "Sorry, what?" she asked, embarrassed that he'd caught her practically undressing Blake with her eyes.

"I asked if you and Blake have known each other long."

"Yeah, a long time. Years and years."

He nodded. "Glad he persuaded you to jump on board."

"Thanks. Me too." Although part of her was already questioning her sanity for doing this to herself.

Best cure for a broken heart was to keep busy and focus on the good things in her life. Soon enough she'd be occupied with her new duties and Blake would be out on various missions, so she wouldn't have the constant reminder of what she couldn't have shoved in her face on a daily basis.

CHAPTER SIX

I slamabad was exactly the same as it had been back in early September: hot, crowded and potentially deadly.

Blake reached out to adjust the vent on the driver's side of the dash board to aim the flow of cool air up to his face. Dunphy was riding shotgun with Zahra and Jordyn in the back of the black SUV. They were second in line behind Alex, Hunter, Claire and Gage. Evers and Tom rode in a third vehicle behind them, along with two Brits hired for additional security. One was a former Royal Marine and the other former SAS. Both had staked out their temporary digs here ahead of time to get everything set up for the taskforce's arrival.

Gage's voice came through Blake's earpiece. "Ready to roll?" he asked from the lead vehicle. Blake and the former SAS member, Lang, replied in the affirmative and the convoy started out from the international airport. They hit traffic almost immediately. It made Blake twitchy as hell to be stuck between other vehicles, but at least they were all in the far right lane so they could get onto the shoulder to make a quick getaway if necessary. Last time he'd been here, he'd witnessed two suicide truck bombings in the downtown core. He and the other drivers were all more than willing to ram cars aside if it came down to it.

"It's worse than L.A.," Dunphy muttered, keeping careful watch out his side of the vehicle for anything suspicious. "And that's saying something."

Yes, it was. Blake kept quiet as Dunphy reached out and plugged his MP3 player in. Two seconds later the sounds of Van Halen filled the interior. "That all you ever listen to?" Blake asked with a shake of his head.

"Why would I listen to anything else?" he answered, sounding genuinely curious.

"Because it gets annoying for the rest of us?" Zahra asked dryly.

"You're just saying that because you're jetlagged and your leg's bugging you," Sean told her. "I won't hold it against you."

Zahra grunted and settled her head back against the headrest. Everyone wore tactical vests. Both women wore shawls to cover their hair, but Jordyn was definitely going to stand out in spite of that. With her height and vivid eyes, locals were going to be shocked to see her carrying a weapon and working on the machinery. She'd barely said a word to him the entire day it'd taken them to get here. Civil and polite, but nothing more. Damn Blake hated it.

Watching her talking and laughing so easily with Evers— the only other single guy on the team—during the flight to Qatar and the long layover there, had stirred something dark and primitive inside him. He'd always felt protective of her but somewhere during the past few years part of him had become possessive of her too. Which was just plain fucked up, since he had no right to be.

Gage's voice came over the earpiece again, yanking him out of his thoughts. "This is going nowhere fast, so I'm getting us outta here. Follow me."

Glad to be moving again, Blake pulled out behind the lead vehicle. He wound his way through the stagnant throng of traffic, ignoring the blare of horns and angry gestures from the other drivers. He bet most of them couldn't say they'd barely escaped back-to-back suicide bombings the last time they'd driven into downtown. Hunter and his now-girlfriend, Khalia, had been the closest when the devices went off. The twin explosions had decimated a crowded government building and a half block of the city. They'd been lucky to walk away from that.

"First time to Pakistan, Zahra?" Jordyn asked in the back seat.

"Yep. Feels weird to be here. I know these are my people but I feel totally out of place. Probably have all kinds of relatives I don't know about right here in the city. Not that I'm going to look any of them up, except maybe someone on my mother's side once this job is done. We'll see."

"Not unless Alex vets them first," Sean said. "I'm not taking any chances with you."

Blake caught Zahra's amused smile in the rearview mirror. "See? He really can be sweet when he drops that clown persona."

"I thought you loved my clown persona?"

"I love *you*," she corrected. "I tolerate the clown because I have no choice."

Sean grinned and went back to doing his job—watching out for possible threats. Driving in a three vehicle convoy like this made them stand out, and that wasn't a good thing. They needed to get to their destination quickly and lie low until they got the next piece of intel that would put them on the trail of Hassani and his network.

"About four klicks north after this," Gage said as he took a right, "then seven klicks west and we'll get back on the highway for a bit."

Gage knew this city almost as well as the locals did, so Blake had no problem following him wherever he wanted to take them. Everyone got quiet again. While David Lee Roth sang about dancing the night away, they took the short cut past the traffic snarl without incident and got back on the highway. Soon enough they reached their exit and looped across the highway toward the building the NSA had secretly commandeered for their headquarters.

The first sign anything was wrong was the plume of smoke that appeared above the crowded group of buildings ahead of them. A minute after that the sound of sirens started up.

They eased over onto the shoulder to let emergency vehicles pass. Warning tingles started in Blake's gut but before he could check in with Gage, Alex came over the earpiece.

"There's a situation near our headquarters. Reports say a motorcycle bomb just went off in that area. We're waiting for confirmation of target and risk assessment. Stand by."

Blake shot a glance at Dunphy, who also wore an earpiece. The man's jaw tightened. Blake looked at Jordyn in the mirror. She was staring out the windshield at the smoke, her expression tense. Even if she hadn't been wearing an earpiece, he knew she'd already figured out something was wrong.

"What's happening?" Zahra asked.

Sean turned in his seat to look at her. "Possible bombing near our building. We're waiting for more info."

Zahra was sitting straight up now, her attention riveted to the rising column of smoke before them. "Is it a welcome message?"

"Don't know," Sean answered, and Blake saw his hand go to the weapon holstered in his waistband. "We'll sit tight until we know more."

But they wouldn't sit here for long.

It made Blake edgy as hell to stay exposed out here, and he knew the others felt the same way. More emergency vehicles flew past them, lights and sirens going. Looked like there might be more damage than he'd initially thought. He shifted in his seat, the weight of his sidearm a comforting presence in its holster against the small of his back. Traffic around them began to build up and the sense of being hemmed in grew to a shrieking awareness inside him.

Finally Alex came back on the team radio. "Ellis," he said to Blake, "we're moving Claire into your vehicle with Zahra. Lang and Wright will drive them east to a different location while the rest of us head in and assess the situation. You guys take their truck. Go."

Dunphy was already unbuckling his belt, explaining the situation to Zahra. Blake turned to face Jordyn in the back seat. She watched him with a steady gaze, her posture tense. "You're switching vehicles with us so we can head up there and take a look."

Without a word she nodded and exited the vehicle, heading around back to pop the tailgate and grab the duffel that held some of their weapons. Blake slid out just as Lang, a sandy blond man in his late thirties, and Wright, a dark haired guy maybe in his mid-twenties, ran up to take over the vehicle.

Blake hurried over to the last vehicle and jumped behind the wheel as Dunphy climbed in beside him and Jordyn slid in next to Tom in the backseat. As soon as they slammed their doors shut Gage took off in the lead with a roar of the engine. Blake followed suit as the Brits moved in behind and took the first right turn, peeling away from the rest of them to take Claire and Zahra to safety just in case.

"What do we know so far?" Tom asked, checking his weapon as Jordyn and Dunphy did the same with their M4s.

"Not much," Blake answered, keeping his attention on the task of following Gage as they veered past the piled up traffic. The police had set up a roadblock ahead to keep traffic and curious onlookers out of the area. He saw Gage handing over documents and talking to the officer there. The Pakistani spoke to someone over the radio then waved both vehicles through.

Once they got close to the scene the level of damage became evident. Gage slowed as they neared the site. The motorcyclist had packed a hell of a lot of explosives into the bomb, because the entire lower face of the building on the corner was gone. Flames poured out of the busted windows and there were still people trapped in the upper floors. Others were carrying the wounded and dead away from the street where the blackened remains of the bike lay smoldering just feet from the curb. Fire crews and paramedics were still arriving on scene.

"Stand by," Alex said. He got out of the lead vehicle and approached the Pakistani officers forming the perimeter around the building as he talked to someone on his cell phone. After a few minutes of talking and questioning the cops, he strode back to the SUV, his voice coming through Blake's earpiece. "Everybody out and take a look around. Let's make sure the area's secure before the bomb squad shows up."

Blake cut the engine and they all gathered on the sidewalk. Jordyn was right next to him, rifle in her hands, gaze moving vigilantly over the growing crowd around them. More than a few people were staring at her, including the Pak cops, because the sight of a woman holding a weapon so comfortably and being part of a male team wasn't something they saw every day. Blake stepped closer to her on instinct, the protective side of him taking over.

Alex divided them into pairs. Blake stayed close to Jordyn as they headed up the near side of the street. They moved together easily, able to anticipate each other's movements because they'd done this sort of exercise dozens of times together for fun back in the day when she was fresh out of bootcamp.

Onlookers lined the streets at the ends where the barricades had been set up. No one made a threatening move at them and nothing suspicious tripped his radar. He and Jordyn stood with their backs to each other as they surveyed the area. "See anything?" he asked.

"Negative. You?"

"Nope." They held their position until Alex spoke over the radio again.

"Witnesses say it was a suicide bomber acting alone. Police confirm that, though they're not ruling out accomplices. They say the bomber detonated his device when he wasn't able to gain access to the restricted section west of here. Making a statement, I guess."

"How close are we to our HQ?" Hunter asked, his voice full of suspicion.

"About three hundred meters. It's the concrete building on the north side to the west."

Blake's head snapped around. Jordyn was already looking in the same direction, zeroed in on the nondescript three-story building in question. *Well, shit.* Talk about too close for comfort.

"This about us?" Dunphy asked, voicing the question they were all thinking.

"That's the million dollar question, isn't it?" Alex said. They all knew Hassani's network had eyes and ears everywhere. Though it was unlikely anyone would have known their headquarters' location already, it was possible someone had noticed the NSA agents setting up the place over the past two days. Someone at immigration might have reported the team's arrival at the airport.

At any rate, they couldn't risk staying here now. Alex let out a hard sigh. "All right, let's move out. We'll go to plan B. Follow us out of here."

He and Jordyn hightailed it back to the guarded SUV with the others. When everyone was loaded up they did a U-turn and headed back through a different barricade. Blake had no idea where they were going, he was just glad Alex had planned for this contingency.

They drove out of the downtown core and took a circuitous route around the city. When they were sure no one was tailing them, Gage led them to the northeastern part of the city, past an industrial district, and pulled through a gate where two well-armed Caucasian men wearing body armor stood guard.

"Home sweet home?" Dunphy deduced from beside Blake.

"Guess so." Blake drove into the open bay garage door and parked next to the other SUV. It was a big space, filled with several motorbikes, a couple ATVs and a beat up piece of shit car that looked like it had fallen down a mountain or two.

Alex slammed his door shut and rounded the hood toward them. "This is where you're going to be working part time," he said to Jordyn. "There're rooms big enough to act as barracks on the upper floor. We'll outfit it so you, Claire and Zahra have one side and the rest of us will take the other." He glanced Blake and Dunphy's way. "Let's get the bunks made up."

So much for the promise of hot showers.

Lang and Wright showed up with Claire and Zahra about thirty minutes into their efforts to make the space liveable for everyone. Wasn't ideal, but it would work for now, until they found better and more secure accommodations. Not that Blake or the other guys would be around much once the intel started rolling in.

By the time they'd brought in bunks for everyone and separated the upper floor in half with two rolling hospital screens to act as a partition, they were all ready to sprawl face first onto their uncomfortable cots and call it a night. Even though it was only two in the afternoon, local time.

Blake found Jordyn down in the garage familiarizing herself with the tools and equipment there. She glanced up from where she'd been organizing a series of socket wrenches and went still when she realized they were alone. She'd taken the shawl off, and he thought again how the short cap of her dark hair made her eyes seem even bigger, bluer.

A pang hit him in the chest at the sight she made there in the midst of that grungy environment. Sexy as hell with those lean feminine lines and curves, her smooth golden skin and soft mouth. He hated that his mind kept going there. Dammit, it shouldn't be this hard to keep his conflicted feelings for her locked down. As he faced her, he barely resisted the urge to rub a hand over the back of his neck. It was too late to say he was sorry for dragging her into this.

Glancing around the garage, he finally found his balls and looked back at her. "You okay with this?"

"Yeah, I'm fine."

Not much of a conversation starter, but then he shouldn't be surprised. She hadn't said a word to him about all the attacks on the team, or about this latest incident that might or might not be connected to them. "Alex'll find us a more secure location in the next few days, but this is a good spot for now. Low key, out of the way." Made it easier for them to stay out of sight for a while.

She nodded.

Damn, what else was he supposed to say? "You need anything?"

Something moved in her eyes, a softness, then she pushed to her feet and crossed toward him, wiping her hands on a rag she'd tucked into her hip pocket. He could tell she was tired, no matter how she tried to hide it. Averting her gaze, she looked down at her hands as she spoke. "Look, I'm not mad at you, okay?"

That was good to know, but it didn't ease his conscience completely. He'd never meant to hurt her—would never hurt her intentionally. "Okay."

Her head came up. She met his eyes for a second then looked away again, as though she couldn't hold his gaze. "I'm not. Seriously, let's just get past this, okay? I'm moving on, promise."

Wait, moving on? "You mean, from the other day, or…?"

She huffed out an annoyed sound. "From everything. The night of the funeral, you, me. Us. Whatever. It's done." She waved a hand dismissively, her cheeks staining bright pink.

Us?

As he dissected that phrase and combined it with the flash of emotion he'd seen in her eyes a minute ago, a flash of realization hit him. *Whoa, wait.* He sucked in a breath, nearly staggered back under the impact of the insight that left him reeling.

Had Jordyn been into him? *Seriously* into him in a way he'd never in a million years suspected, let alone given himself permission to even dream about?

Blake searched her face, needing to know for certain that's what she'd just implied. Looking back now, he realized he might not have imagined the longing and wistfulness he'd seen in her eyes during his last few visits with her family.

Oh, Jesus. He swallowed, aware that his heart was thudding against his chest wall. "I never thought—I didn't realize you…" He trailed off, not knowing what the hell to say or what to think, and blurting out useless shit would only make things worse.

He'd known she'd had a crush on him for a while, but never thought it meant anything. Had it been way more than that to her? For the first time he allowed himself to examine and admit his long-buried feelings for her. A wave of regret slammed into him. He fucking worshipped the ground she walked on. Thought she was talented, smart and funny, loyal and sexy as hell.

She cocked her head at him, narrowed her eyes in suspicion. "What, you thought I was just looking for a fuck buddy that night?"

He didn't answer, because that's exactly what he'd thought. The night of Jamie's funeral, he'd mistakenly assumed she'd been acting out of grief and loneliness, turning to him to make the pain stop and nothing more.

He still couldn't comprehend the magnitude of all this; that she'd wanted more than sex. Evidently a *hell* of a lot more. The Marine Corps had trained him to be an elite observer, an expert on noticing things about people most others didn't. So how the hell had he missed the signs of how she'd felt about him? Or had he just not *let* himself see them?

He ran a hand over his hair, suddenly realizing just how badly he'd fucked this up.

When he didn't respond, she snorted and shook her head at him in disgust. "God, you're such a jackass."

No, he was a total fucking *idiot*. "I had no idea you thought of me that way." It was true. But a primal leap of triumph swept through his veins at her admission. He knew Jordyn. Knew she didn't give her heart easily, and when she did, she gave it wholeheartedly. That devastated look on her face when he'd told her why he'd dropped out of her life? It made all kinds of sense now. God.

But that unease still twisted inside him, the one that warned she wasn't for him and that he'd be stupid to risk his heart that way again.

"Yeah, got that loud and clear. So, can we move on now?" Her eyes blazed with anger and pride, her cheeks bright pink. "Whatever, like I said, I'm over it. Let's just both be adults and deal with it. Fresh start, beginning now." She turned away and took a step toward the door.

"Wait." He shot out a hand and grabbed her forearm in a firm grip. Not hard enough to hurt, but hard enough that she'd have to use force to get free.

She paused and turned her head toward him slightly but didn't meet his eyes. "What?" she snapped, tension rolling off her in waves.

He so wasn't having this conversation with her back to him.

He tugged her around to face him and waited, letting the silence stretch out until she was forced to meet his gaze. Her guard was up; he could see it in the rigid set of her shoulders and the tension around her mouth and eyes.

Blake shook his head, feeling awed and devastated at the same time. He should have told her all this months ago. "I've felt guilty as shit for even *thinking* about you as anything but a friend, let alone the way I have for the past three years, and you're telling me now that all this time you've wanted more?" Every time he'd thought about anything other than a platonic relationship with her, he'd instantly shoved the feelings into a bombproof box deep inside him and locked it there. Hell, he'd felt guilty as fuck for fantasizing about her the way he had.

She blinked, her mouth dropping open before she managed to cover her shock. "Why would you feel guilty?"

Seriously? "Jesus, Jordyn, you were like a *sister* to me. For *years*. You know how important your parents are to me and that I'd never do anything to jeopardize my relationship with them, just like I would never do anything that might risk losing you." He wasn't even sure when his feelings for her had started to change, he just knew they had a few years back and he'd been damn careful to keep it from both her and Jamie. Fuck, even from himself half the time.

Her eyes widened. "That's why you stayed away after the funeral? Because you felt guilty about wanting me and worried what my *parents* would think?"

Why did she look so incredulous about that, and did she have to make it sound so stupid? Couldn't she see the inherent risks involved if he'd done otherwise? The consequences if he'd slept with her that night and things hadn't worked out afterward? He scrubbed a hand over his face and released her arm. Thankfully, she didn't storm off and leave him there.

He struggled to organize his chaotic thoughts. Talking about his feelings was torture, but this was way worse. "First off, I didn't know you had those kinds of feelings for me."

"Oh, please."

"I didn't. I thought it was just a crush or something and that you'd gotten over it a while ago."

She snorted like he'd just insulted her in the worst manner possible. "A crush, Blake? Like I'm still a stupid teenager or something? Yeah, *no*. Not even close."

Then what do you feel? he wanted to blurt out. It was hell to be this close to what he wanted and not know what her true feelings were, even if it was too soon to demand that of her. He itched to touch her, reach out and cup the smooth curve of her cheek in his hand, rub his thumb over that satiny skin. To be the one to take that first step over the wall between them.

Instead, he held himself in check and forced out the rest of it. "Second, what if we did get together, then things didn't work out and you wound up hating me? Then I'd lose you and your family too."

Rather than appear offended, she frowned as if she couldn't understand his thought process. "Why do you assume things wouldn't work out? We've got a hell of a lot more in common than any other couple I know, and we've been friends for years. I know you better than anyone."

All true. But she knew exactly why. Fuck, his heart was pounding like he'd been running for miles. "Jamie would have lost his shit over this."

"Well, he's not here, is he? And you're wrong. He might've been shocked or even mad at first, but unless you were planning on just fucking me and walking away, I know he'd have approved of us being together."

"You think I'd do that?" he demanded, outraged that she'd think so little of him. "You damn well better know I wouldn't. That's why I stopped things before they got out of hand—" He broke off with a frustrated sigh. He'd given Jamie his word he'd look out for Jordyn. Blake was pretty sure an adult—very adult—relationship wasn't what Jamie'd had in mind. He felt like he was standing on the edge of a precipice, and whatever came next would change his life forever.

Hope and need rose inside him at the word *together*, twin bubbles expanding in his chest until it was hard to breathe. "You're not worried at all about screwing things up?"

Her eyes frosted a little. "No. I'm not Melissa, in case you haven't noticed."

The mention of that name didn't sting the way it used to, but he still hid a wince at the sharp edge in her tone. "I know." He was well aware that Jordyn was nothing like his ex-fiancée. And besides, his feelings for her were totally different from what he'd felt for Melissa. He'd been young and naive back then, too blinded by heat and lust and fireworks to realize that what they had was merely the appearance of a relationship wrapped in a sexy package.

One that had quickly fallen apart at the seams during his first long deployment. As proof, he'd received the Dear John e-mail four months in. A fucking e-mail to end their engagement, for God's sake.

"I never liked her," Jordyn added, folding her arms across her chest.

He huffed out a laugh. "I know you didn't." She'd made no secret of that, hadn't even tried to be friendly to Melissa when he'd brought her to the Bridgers' house for two weekend visits before they'd gotten engaged.

Jordyn shook her head. "You should've listened to me when I told you she wasn't good enough for you."

"Yeah, I know that too." Although if he had, he wouldn't have learned the valuable lessons he'd learned from the experience, painful though they'd been. After the devastation and heartache had eased enough for him to take a hard look at things, he'd realized he was mourning the loss of something that had only ever existed in his imagination. In hindsight, what he'd had with Melissa was so superficial he couldn't believe he'd ever thought they could make a marriage work.

This pull between him and Jordyn went far deeper than anything he'd felt before. Their bond was grounded in admiration and the solidity of more than a decade of friendship. Wasn't that what real love was supposed to be based on? All he knew was, the thought of her with another man made him jealous as fuck. And if anyone ever hurt her the way Melissa had hurt him, he'd happily hunt them down and rip their limbs off for her.

"God, I hated her for what she did to you," Jordyn continued. "We all did. Don't let her actions affect the rest of your life."

He nodded, still struggling to come to grasp with everything she'd said, though he appreciated her calling him on his bullshit. He'd spent nearly two years chasing after a figment of his imagination when the real thing had been right there in front of him the whole time. There was a certain bittersweet irony in that.

But Jordyn was here now. Standing right here, close enough to touch. And she wanted him. Was he dreaming all this? He let everything wash through him, the pent-up need, the longing. Unable to hold back a second longer, Blake reached out and cradled the side of her face, savoring the feel of that silky soft skin against his palm. His blood thrummed heavily through his veins when she sucked in a sharp breath and stared up at him with that mixture of hope and need that tied him in knots.

"So what now?" he asked softly, rubbing his thumb gently across her cheekbone. "What do you want?"

"You. That's it, Blake. There's no riddle to decipher, no code to break. I want *you*." Staring deep into his eyes, she reached up and wrapped her fingers around his wrist, holding him there while she rubbed her cheek against his palm. The tenderness in the gesture turned his heart over.

Lust and satisfaction blasted through him. The painful pressure in his chest eased, relief sweeping aside the doubt and uncertainty. His gaze dropped to her mouth, a silent groan rumbling up inside him when her little pink tongue stole out to lick across her lower lip in a quick, almost nervous motion. Tightening his hand on her face, he wrapped his other arm around her waist and pulled her in close, until only an inch or two of space separated them. "I want you too," he murmured, and kissed her.

Jordyn let out a soft whimper and grabbed the back of his head with her free hand, the other still locked around his wrist. But he wasn't going anywhere. Not when he finally had her willing and in his arms again. He took his time kissing her, exploring the shape of her mouth with his lips and tongue. Last time had been desperate and fueled by grief and longing. This time it was slower, softer. Hotter because of the raging fire burning between them.

She opened to the caress of his tongue and leaned fully against him, those small, firm breasts he'd fantasized about for so many nights now pressed to his chest. His arm contracted around her waist, his other hand sliding into her hair to hold her still as he licked and caressed the inside of her mouth. Her sweet scent and taste filled him, made his erection throb painfully against the front of his cargo pants. She eased forward until her pelvis pressed against him, the pressure a sweet torture.

They both heard the footsteps in the stairway at the same time.

Mentally swearing, Blake reluctantly lifted his head and eased away. Jordyn stepped back, breathing as hard as him, her lips pink and shiny and her face flushed, those gorgeous eyes glowing with unfulfilled arousal. He drank it all in and envisioned her spread out for him on a wide bed, naked, her eyes holding that exact same look as he held her arms above her head and buried himself inside her as deep as he could go.

Dunphy emerged through the doorway. His greeting smile faded a little as he looked back and forth between the two of them. "Am I interrupting?"

"No, of course not," Jordyn blurted, turning back to the bike she'd been working on and picking up a screwdriver.

Dunphy raised an eyebrow at Blake. "Sure?"

"Yeah, we're sure," he snapped. "What's up?" As in, *what the hell do you want?*

"Alex wants us to hit the range to zero our scopes."

That helped clear the lust-tinged fog clouding Blake's brain. "He get new intel or something?"

"Think so. Wants us up and ready to move the moment he gets word, so he wants this out of the way." He leaned his head to the side to see behind Blake. "You too, Jordyn. We're heading out in ten minutes, so grab your gear."

"Okay." She seemed as surprised by the order as Blake was, and shared a questioning look with him. "I'll just get my rifle."

As she jogged up the stairs, Blake strode across to the other side of the warehouse to start collecting his equipment. "What's he want Jordyn there for?" If she was filling a support role, then why did she need to zero her weapon?

"Dunno, and didn't ask him. You *sure* I didn't interrupt anything? Because it sure as hell looked like I did. And whatever it was, from how flushed her face was, it must have been *hot*."

Blake stopped what he was doing to look back at Dunphy, not liking the teasing glint he saw in the other man's eyes.

Not when it was about something involving Jordyn that could potentially damage her reputation on the team. "You didn't see shit, Dunphy. And if you say anything to hurt her reputation, you'll deal with me."

The other eyebrow rose to join the first at Blake's warning tone. "Wow, it's like that, huh? Good for you, and it's about damn time, man. My lips are sealed."

Doubtful, Blake thought sourly as he turned back to his work. Now he not only had to worry about keeping his hands off Jordyn, he had to make sure the sudden shift in their relationship stayed a secret until this job was over.

★ ★ ★

CHAPTER SEVEN

"**B**ring him in."

One of Malik's bodyguards opened the door and the other pushed the guest inside. A tall, thin man with a twitch in his lips when he was nervous. Right now he was more than nervous. His face had a sheen of sweat on it and his movements were stiff and jerky as he moved fully into the room.

Switching his attention from the man, Malik nodded at his guards, who shut the door. They'd stand just on the other side of it in the hallway and await further instructions. Which would be coming within a few minutes, if he had to guess. From the agitated state his visitor was in, this shouldn't take long at all.

"Please, sit." Not a polite invitation, but a quiet order.

The man understood because he immediately dropped into the chair Malik had indicated and clasped his hands in his lap. The knuckles were white with tension, those thin fingers fidgeting restlessly. "Whatever it is they told you I've done, they're lying."

Ah. In his experience, an admission of innocence before being charged with anything was usually an indication of guilt. Not that Malik was surprised the man was lying. "Is that so?"

The man nodded adamantly. "Yes. I haven't done anything."

"Have you not?"

"No. I would never cross you. Never."

"And why is that?"

"Because I know how..." He paused, seemed to collect himself before licking his lips and continuing. "Your reputation."

Malik smiled, amused by the comment. "Really. And what reputation do I have?"

Those frantic, dark eyes widened a fraction, then the gaze dropped away. Another signal of guilt. "That your enemies all...disappear."

"And do you believe such stories?"

His throat moved in a nervous swallow. "Yes."

Malik pushed away from his desk. "Then that makes me wonder why you would take such a risk by talking with an American spy."

The man paled visibly, every muscle in his body going rigid. "I didn't—"

"You *did*." Malik's temper surged, dark and dangerous. Did this waste of skin think Malik was stupid? It had been a long time since he'd killed one of his enemies personally, but he was tempted to do so now. Being so close to his goal only to suffer a setback because of weak, spineless men like this was too much to bear.

"No, I—"

Malik cut off whatever further protests he was going to make by pulling the photos from his pocket and tossing them on the floor at the man's feet. Pictures showing him speaking to a man connected to Alex Rycroft.

No response, other than a look of horror and the absolute silence that permeated the room.

"I know what you did. I even know what you said." Malik edged closer until he was towering over the man, the tips of his shoes a mere inch from the scuffed brown boots. "You know what that makes you?"

Again no response. Malik knew exactly how to play this, just what to do to make a prisoner squirm until they broke. He let the silence fill the room, until it grew so huge that it seemed to press against the walls.

Finally that stricken gaze lifted to his.

Malik leaned down until their noses nearly touched and stared right into the man's terrified eyes. "That makes you my enemy."

At the quiet, deadly edge to his tone, that thin frame started shaking. The man's face crumpled and he burst into noisy tears. "Please."

Disgusted, Malik whirled away and called for his guard.

"Please! I had to talk, they were going to arrest me for being connected with you. I didn't tell them much, only—"

"Shut up." The barked command silenced the sniveling immediately. His bodyguards stepped inside and looked to him for instructions. "Take him away and deal with him," he ordered in a flat tone, flicking a dismissive hand toward the crying man. He tuned out the desperate pleas and the tears, even the screams as his guards dragged the man out to where a vehicle would be waiting. They'd drive the prisoner out into the desert and shoot him. A much kinder death than he deserved, Malik thought, his hands curling into fists.

He bent to pick up the scattered color photographs and shoved them back into his pocket to be disposed of later. Knowing that traitor would never see another sunrise helped ease the anger somewhat. When a knock came a minute later, he was calm again.

At his command, Bashir entered the room. "A call for you, from a concerned friend." He handed over what Malik knew had to be an encrypted phone.

He answered, unsurprised when he heard the familiar voice of his current ISI contact coming through the phone. "That problem I mentioned last night. Have you fixed it?"

The sound of an engine starting came from outside. "Just."

"I have more news. They're here."

The Americans. A slow smile spread across Malik's face. "Since when?"

"Just since this afternoon. They're not staying where we anticipated, however. And the welcoming committee blew the surprise early." To anyone overhearing the conversation, nothing either of them had said should trigger suspicion.

Malik understood the message, however. The bomber had not only missed the target, he'd detonated his device early. "Where are they?"

"Right now, I have no idea. If I hear anything I'll let you know, but I thought it best you knew this now so you can make other arrangements."

To get out of the country. "Yes, thank you." He disconnected and looked at Bashir. "We're crossing the border tonight. Get everything ready. I have a call to make."

"Yes, sir."

Alone in the windowless room, he contacted an ally up in the mountains, fully aware that the call would trigger the start of the end for either him or the Americans here to hunt him.

Bent over inspecting another problem she'd just discovered with the bike, Jordyn glanced up when footsteps sounded on the concrete steps leading down from the barracks on the second floor. Combat boots and a pair of long, muscular legs clad in cargo pants came into view, followed by a muscular torso in a light gray T-shirt. Her heart was already beating faster and then Blake's face appeared in the doorway.

He smiled when he saw her, and that combination of heat and affection set off a somersault low in her abdomen. She hadn't seen him since late yesterday afternoon, when they'd all grabbed a bite to eat together after hitting the range. She'd almost forgotten how sexy it was to see him shoot. It was like he became part of the gun somehow. So calm, beautiful and deadly.

But mostly that smile made her think about their kiss yesterday. Her toes curled in her steel-toed boots as she remembered the hunger in his embrace, the caress of his tongue. "Hey."

"Hey." He gestured to the bike, propped on its side on the work table. "Figure out what's wrong with it?"

"Might be easier to ask if I'd found what *isn't* wrong with it." She set down her needle-nosed pliers next to a row of spark plugs she'd just taken out and cleaned. "Lot of corrosion on most of the parts I've pulled out, and I've got to replace the fuel line on this one. The other one's in slightly better shape, but not by much. Where the hell did Alex find these, anyway? The junkyard?"

"Never know with him. He's resourceful." He eyed the bike doubtfully for a second. "Can you fix it?"

"Think so. Just hope Alex doesn't plan to use them much, because I'm not sure if they'll stay running for very long, even if I do get them all back together."

"Need a hand?"

She smiled, glad for the offer and for the chance to spend more time alone with him. Not that she expected a repeat of yesterday since someone could walk in at any moment—probably a good thing because she didn't think she'd be able to stop once she put her hands on him again. But a girl could dream. "Sure, that'd be great."

They worked together in silence for a while, his nearness a constant reminder of how that long, strong body had felt up against hers. The way he'd held her had made her feel so wanted and cherished, and the stroke of his tongue against hers made her nipples tighten just to remember it.

He passed her tools and helped when she asked him to. Just like old times around the shop, only sweeter now that she knew she was finally more than Jamie's little sister to him. "You guys were all up and gone early," she commented as she tightened a bolt. "Anything interesting happen?"

"Just some recon and surveillance with the guys."

He didn't come right out and say they were following up on leads to Hassani, but she knew that's what they'd been doing. "Any more word on that bombing yesterday?"

He lowered the socket wrench he'd been using and lifted his eyes to hers. "Some."

She raised a brow and waited, knowing that pressing him for more wouldn't make him give up anything he wasn't supposed to. That was another thing she admired about Blake—the man was a vault when it came to keeping secrets. While she had the security clearance, she knew what her role was here and that she wouldn't always be privy to what was going on with the overall operation.

"Word is the bomber was linked to the TTP cell Hassani backs. Somehow the network found out we were setting up shop in the area, but didn't know the exact location, and when the bomber couldn't get through the barricade he detonated to make a statement."

Though she'd been expecting it, his answer was confirmation enough and it set off a pang of dread inside her. "Well, good thing we've got Wright and Lang to keep an eye out for us while the rest of you are gone."

"Then there's you and Evers too," he pointed out.

"Yup, can't forget me and Evers." The Fed had been working with Claire and Zahra all last night and this morning on new leads, and the two Brits seemed like solid operators. Still, it bothered her to be in such an isolated place with so little protection. When she'd served in the Corps she'd always been in the relative safety of a base with plenty of protection and firepower around. She reached for a Phillips head screwdriver, but paused when Blake wrapped his warm fingers around her hand.

His touch sent tingles radiating up her arm and throughout the rest of her. It was hard to remember why she was so anxious when all she could think about at that moment was those hands all over her naked body the way she'd always imagined. He stared right into her eyes as he spoke. "You're safe here. I'd never leave you here alone if I didn't believe that, and Alex is even more vigilant about our setup now than he was before."

It was sweet of him to try to reassure her. "I worry about you too, you know." He'd be going out hunting for real soon enough, as soon as they got their first solid piece of intel that might lead to Hassani. She knew he could hold his own better than most out there, but that didn't mean she wasn't still worried as hell about him.

At that he grinned and squeezed her hand once before releasing her. "I kinda like knowing you worry about me."

She laughed and picked up her tool. "You would. Now hand me that box end wrench and help me with this damn thing." Before she decided to say to hell with it and grabbed him by those broad shoulders for another knee-melting kiss. Not an easy feat, to hold back. She'd waited forever for the man to realize she was the one. He was pure, sinful distraction.

They'd just managed to get the engine together and were preparing to replace the fuel line when Alex strode in. He nodded at them in greeting and focused that sharp silver gaze on her. "Can I drag you away from that for a while?"

She put down her tools and began wiping her hands on a shop towel. "Sure, what do you need?"

"Want you to come check out another vehicle with me. Ellis, grab Dunphy and do another drive-by of that last location," he said to Blake.

Jordyn spared him a glance and a quick smile as he left. She grabbed her tactical vest and followed Alex out the side door into the bright sunlight. "Should I go grab my head scarf?" She was already armed, her pistol tucked into its holster at the back of her waistband.

"I wouldn't bother," he said, pulling on his own vest as he strode for the SUV parked next to the building. "Just leave your cap on."

Worked for her. She slid into the front passenger seat and rode shotgun. They drove for nearly twenty minutes outside the city limits before Alex turned off the main road and headed for what looked like another good-sized town. He drove up to some sort of an impound lot and parked.

"What are we looking for?" she asked.

"Contact of mine in the Pak government set aside some more wheels for us. Wanted to get a second opinion on it before I say yes. I told them I was bringing the best mechanic on our team, so they're expecting us."

At his signal she got out and followed him to the chain link fence where an armed guard stood watch. He conversed with the guard briefly in what she assumed must be Urdu, then the guy handed over a set of keys and waved them through. He did a double take and took a closer look at her and she realized he'd only just figured out that she was a woman. The curiosity and shock on his face gave her pause but he merely stared at her so she ignored him and followed Alex inside the lot.

Parked near the end of the fifth row of vehicles sat a newer, dark blue SUV. "This is it." Alex unlocked it and popped the hood then opened all the doors and the rear hatch. "Take a look at the engine and make sure everything's as it should be, while I check out the rest of it."

"Why's it in the impound lot, and why do we want it?"

"It's a gesture of goodwill, Jordyn." Something in his tone told her he was teasing her, but she didn't know him well enough to be certain.

She twisted her ball cap around to sit backwards on her head and leaned in to get a better look beneath the hood. The sun was high, nearly directly overhead, and the heat radiated up off the black asphalt in scorching waves. Brushing the back of her hand across her sweaty forehead, she set her hands on the edge of the frame. As far as engines went, this one looked brand new. She poked around and checked everything out but it all looked fine. Only way to tell if something was wrong was to fire it up and listen.

"It all looks good to me." Too good. Weird that a vehicle like this was dumped here amidst a lot of scrap cars. Very few in the lot appeared to be in this kind of condition. Alex was still looking around in back. She ducked her head under the hood once more and something caught her eye. In the shadows cast by the hood it was hard to see it, but... "Hey, you got a flashlight or anything?"

Alex popped up and came around the front of the vehicle to hand her his keys with a tiny pen light attached to the chain. "What've you got?"

"Not sure, but there's something right down here, in between the..." She paused as her fingers hit something solid and rectangular wedged in beside the engine block. Frowning, she angled the light toward it and tried to get a better look. "I can't see it from here. Can you check from underneath?"

Alex got on his back and shimmied beneath the SUV. "Where?" he asked, and this time there was a decidedly urgent note in his voice.

"Here, against the side of the frame. Can you see my fingers?"

"Hand me the pen light." When she did, he shined it upward. "Okay, I see your hand. Move it just an inch or so to your left." Doing as he said, her heart rate kicked up a notch when he let out a low, "Fuck. Me."

"What?" She wasn't sure why she was whispering, since it was only the two of them here and the guard was too far away to hear their conversation.

Rather than answer and confirm her suspicion, Alex slid out from beneath the vehicle and dusted himself off, his expression now hard. Icy. "Well, at least we've got a new lead to follow up on."

Oh, shit. "Is it a bomb?"

"Yep. Stay here." Without waiting for her to respond he stalked over to where the guard stood watching them. She didn't dare move from her spot but reached a hand back to wrap her fingers around the grip of her pistol and kept her attention riveted on the guard. If he made a move to reach for his own weapon she could drop him easily from here.

After a few minutes of heated conversation filled with much angry gesturing and raised voices, Alex strode back toward her, the babbling guard in tow. Whatever it was he was saying, he stopped when Alex dragged him beneath the vehicle and showed him the device. They emerged into the sunlight a few moments later, Alex looking more pissed off than ever, and the guard sweaty and pale. Once the guard trotted off to the guard house, Alex turned his attention to her.

"Let's unhook it and get outta here."

She blinked. Just like that? "Are we still taking the vehicle?" She eyed it with trepidation. God only knew what other kinds of booby traps there might be in there.

"Nah, I got what I wanted. Let's get this thing out." He cast her a sideways look as he leaned over the engine. "Ever done this before?"

She had some experience with demolitions, but not with car bombs. "No."

"This one's pretty unsophisticated. No trip wires or anything else to worry about." He sounded damn near insulted by that. "We just have to unhook the leads and get it out of there. Hold the light for me?" He handed her back the pen light.

Shining it so he could see what he was doing, Jordyn watched closely as Alex dug a pocketknife out of his pants and flipped out a little screwdriver attachment. He unhooked the wires from the battery terminals then checked to make sure he hadn't missed anything before he got down on the ground on his back and wedged himself beneath the undercarriage. "Man, they wedged this in good and tight," he said with a grunt as he wrestled to pull the plastic explosives out of its hiding spot.

"My hands are smaller. Want me to try?"

"Yeah." He pulled out and dusted himself off, seeming totally unconcerned that someone had planted explosives in the vehicle they were supposed to have taken. If she'd started the engine, it likely would have detonated. The thought made her go cold all over.

She handed him the pen light and got under the vehicle. It took a while for her to work the Semtex free but eventually it gave way and she was able to push it upward so Alex could pull it out from beneath the engine block.

He helped her up. "Let's head back. The guys and I have more work to do now." He was already on his phone texting something as he walked away.

Feeling more than a little unsettled, Jordyn followed him back to their SUV and did a thorough sweep of it with him before climbing inside. Once they were on the road, she couldn't keep the questions inside any longer. "You said the Pakistani government earmarked that for us."

"Yep." He drove with his left arm propped on the window frame, utterly at ease.

"So does that mean someone in the government planted that, hoping to kill us?"

"That's the way I read it, yeah."

The nonchalant tone was really starting to grate on her nerves. She blew out a breath. "And we're not going to do anything about that?"

He glanced over at her, his silver eyes intense, penetrating. "Hell yeah, we are."

Realization slowly dawned. "You suspected they'd done this?" Someone or something must have tipped him off earlier, which was why he'd wanted to check it out personally. He'd not only anticipated this, clearly he'd had a plan in mind for when he confirmed the evidence. But there was still something that didn't make any sense to her at all. "And you wanted me to come along because…?"

"Because if it was hidden under the hood, I knew you'd be able to find it faster than me. You were a big help, thanks." He clapped a hand on her shoulder twice.

She forced her gaze away from him to stare out the windshield. "You're um, welcome."

One thing was for sure; she may have spent her entire life surrounded by military men, but she'd never, ever met a man like Alex Rycroft before.

CHAPTER EIGHT

The call to evening prayer had just sounded from the minarets of the local mosque when Blake arrived back at HQ with Dunphy. Hunter and Gage were already inside after a five hour recon job that had turned up exactly nothing. Everyone was wiped and looking forward to some quality rack time.

Except for him, because from the muted sounds coming from the garage, he knew Jordyn was still working. He found her tackling the second bike, the first now parked next to the closed rolling bay door. She had her ball cap on backward.

She stopped what she was doing when he entered, her welcoming smile doing funny things to his heart. Even dressed in cargo pants and a T-shirt and wearing no makeup, she was still the hottest woman he'd ever known. He couldn't wait to finally stroke all those long, lean lines, find out where she was most sensitive and use it to drive her out of her mind.

"Just get back?" she asked, coming around the end of the workbench toward him.

"A few minutes ago." The warmth and obvious affection in her eyes were just for him and knowing that made him feel like the luckiest sonofabitch in the world. When she stepped up to wrap her arms around him he tugged her close and buried his face in her neck. Her little sigh of pleasure and contentment tangled him up inside, had his body tightening in need. God, she felt good up against him. She fit perfectly in his hold, all soft and pliant. The mixed scents of shampoo, soap and a hint of axel grease teased his nostrils. Pure Jordyn.

He smiled against her neck and nuzzled the velvety skin just below her ear, earning a delicate shiver from her. He'd never been free to express what he'd truly felt for her before. He was going to savor every moment of this stolen time together. "What about you? How long you been in here?"

"Since Alex and I got back a few hours ago," she murmured into his shoulder. She cuddled in closer, apparently content to stay right where she was and Blake was only too happy to hold her close like this. His whole body felt electrically charged, every nerve ending attuned to each place they touched.

She lifted her head. Her eyes were smoky with desire. One he couldn't wait for the chance to satisfy. But not here where they had no privacy. When he took her, it would be somewhere behind a locked door when they had enough time to explore each other so he could find out exactly how to ramp her up until she was begging for him to fuck her.

"Did he tell you what happened?" she asked.

The fog of lust cleared slightly from his brain. "No, what?" He stroked a hand up her back, the other wrapped securely around her waist. If she felt this good with her clothes on, he couldn't wait to find out what she'd feel like naked against him. Beneath him, on top of him, he didn't care, but whenever it finally happened he planned to show her all the things he'd been fantasizing about with her.

He knew she was thinking about the exact same thing because she squirmed against him and seemed to shake herself before answering. "We went to this impound lot to look at a vehicle the government had set aside for us. Alex told me to check the engine, and when I did we found this." She pulled away from him and walked over to a box on a shelf anchored to the wall. When she reached inside and held up a block of Semtex with the wires and blasting caps still attached, his eyes widened.

"Holy shit." He took it from her and examined it. "Was it hooked up to the battery?"

"Yeah, but whoever planted this did a good job of hiding it. And it was a bitch to get out of there once Alex unhooked it."

He looked up into her eyes. "What did he say?"

"I think he knew it was there all along. He's been busy with Evers and the girls from the time we got back, I think following up on the potential lead this gives us. He mentioned something about having Claire trace the material or whatever. Then he could maybe find out where it had come from and who authorized planting it. I'm guessing someone in the police or military, but I'm not sure." She frowned. "He really didn't say anything?"

"No, nothing." Not that it surprised him, knowing what a secretive bastard Alex was. Blake set the plastic explosive aside, just grateful they'd found it before they'd fired up the engine. If it had gone off, it would've killed them and probably anyone else within a fifty yard radius. He studied her intently, searching for signs of fear or strain but saw nothing that concerned him except the lines of fatigue around her eyes and mouth. Lifting a hand, he traced the shadows under her eyes. "You must be wiped."

She leaned into his touch, that spark of desire igniting in her eyes once more. "Yeah, the jetlag's starting to catch up with me. I'll head up once I'm finished cleaning these spark plugs." She had a row of them laid out on top of the bench. "What about you?"

"I'm free right now, so I'll give you a hand." Though he wanted to haul her close and kiss her until she couldn't breathe, he didn't want to start anything he couldn't finish and the sooner he could help her finish up, the better. They both needed sleep.

He reached for a plug, started scrubbing at the rust with a rag drenched in cleaner but paused when someone knocked on the side door. He opened it to find Alex there, that usual air of barely suppressed energy humming around him.

"Hey, wanted to give you both a heads up that we might have a solid lead to follow. Better crash for a bit while you can, because once we get a location, we're outta here."

"Got it," Blake replied. He shut the door behind Alex and turned to face Jordyn. "You gonna head up now?"

She sighed. "Guess we'd better. I'll finish this first thing in the morning."

Blake wasn't leaving her without staking his claim one more time.

In three easy strides he stood in front of her. She stared up at him, waiting, those gorgeous eyes darkening as her pupils expanded. Taking her face in his hands, he caught her quiet gasp as he trailed a line of kisses from her forehead and down her nose, then at last covered her mouth with his. She twined her arms around his neck and lifted up on tiptoe to kiss him back, her tongue darting out to play with his.

Blake bit back a groan at the taste of her, sweet and hot with a hint of cinnamon like she'd been eating candy before he walked in. Need clawed at him. He wanted to see the expression on her face as he touched and tasted her everywhere. Wanted to see her eyes go blind when he put his mouth between her legs and teased her with his tongue.

He was rock hard in his cargo pants, the length of his erection pressing against the softness of her abdomen. His whole body pulsed as the heat exploded between them. Then Jordyn made it a thousand times worse by rubbing against him, a little moan of pleasure and need escaping her.

With a low growl, Blake shoved her ball cap off. He fisted his hands in her soft, short hair, showing her exactly how much he wanted her. Needed her. If he'd thought they wouldn't be interrupted, he would have started peeling off her clothes just to see and touch all that silky skin hidden from his ravenous gaze. But this place gave them only the illusion of privacy and he would never jeopardize Jordyn's reputation by being careless. If anyone caught them he didn't want it to look like she wasn't taking her job seriously, or that they were having a fling just because they both had an itch to scratch.

Breathing hard, his heart racing, he forced himself to end the kiss. For a moment her arms tightened about his neck in protest, then she pressed her face into his chest, taking slow, deep breaths to calm herself. "How'm I gonna sleep now that you've got me all wound up again?" she muttered against his shirt.

Hell if he knew. He'd be up half the night with a painful hard on now. Releasing his grip on her hair, he wrapped his arms around her back and squeezed tight. "I don't wanna let you go, angel."

Her head came up at the endearment, those big blue eyes searching his, full of unquenched need. "I'm not going anywhere, Blake. I've waited a long time for this. For you."

God, she turned him inside out when she said things like that. He hated leaving her all worked up and unsatisfied. "If I get called out, I'll keep in touch as much as I can."

She nodded, but he could see the worry lingering in her eyes. "I'll be here when you get back."

The primal part of him fucking loved knowing she'd be waiting for him. "Take care of yourself, okay?"

"I will. You too."

Before he gave in to the need to say to hell with his restraint and finish what they'd started, he released her and set a hand on her lower back to usher her toward the stairs. And if he stared at her ass the entire time she climbed them, who could blame him? It was a damn fine ass. At the top she looked over her shoulder at him and gave a sexy little smile that set his libido racing before she entered the female quarters.

All revved up with no end to his torment in sight, Blake walked down the hall, eased the door to the men's side of the barracks open and crept inside. There was barely enough light for him to make out the rows of inflatable mattresses laid out on the floor. He stopped and squinted when he saw Dunphy crouching next to Gage's bunk. Hunter, Alex and Evers were all gone. Dunphy swung his head around to glance at him, held a finger up to his lips to signal for silence, then turned back to whatever he was doing.

As his eyes adjusted to the dimness, Blake saw the scene more clearly as he headed for his own bunk. Dunphy was perched on his haunches behind Gage's head, a grin of gleeful anticipation on his face as he knelt over his unsuspecting victim. He was holding something in his hand. Gage was out cold, one tatted arm folded beneath his head, the other stretched out over the edge of the mattress, palm up. A tall pile of what had to be shaving cream lay in the center of it.

Blake shook his head at Dunphy. *Dude, seriously?* And picking on the exhausted, oldest guy on the team whose hearing still hadn't recovered from injuries sustained in the line of duty a few weeks back? Dunphy must be desperate to have a little fun to pick Gage as a target.

Unperturbed by the audience or Blake's silent disapproval, Dunphy leaned down and carefully brushed something across Gage's face. The second-in-command twitched in his sleep but didn't wake, his nearly unconscious state telling Blake how smoked he was.

Not that Dunphy cared. No, he let out a quiet snicker and did it again, dragging what looked like a piece of string or something over Gage's bristly face. This time the former master sergeant felt it and instinctively brought his hand up to brush the tickling thing away, covering his face in shaving cream in the process.

Jolting awake, Gage let out an outraged roar and vaulted from the air mattress. Dunphy barked out a laugh and scrambled out of the way, cackling like a lunatic. The sound of it was so infectious, Blake couldn't help but laugh too.

Gage didn't find it nearly so amusing. He locked onto Dunphy with a ferocious glower. "What the fuck is wrong with you, man?" he bellowed, swiping at the white foam smeared all over him.

"Couldn't help it," Dunphy wheezed between peals of laughter. "It was t-too good an opportunity to p-pass up." He doubled over and howled some more, wiping the tears of mirth from his eyes.

"Fuck you." Gage shot Blake a pissed off glare for good measure and stalked off in the direction of the bathroom. "Pain in my fucking ass, Dunphy," he said over his shoulder.

"Not as big as the pain you gave my ass last week," Dunphy called out, and earned a raised middle finger from Gage just before he slammed the bathroom door behind him and locked it for good measure.

"Mess with the bull, you get the horns," Blake told his spotter as he stripped his pants off and slid under the covers.

"Nah, it's all in fun. He was out so deep, I just couldn't help myself. He's been in such a piss poor mood ever since we got here, I figured I should lighten things up a bit."

Well, no wonder. "On top of everything else he's worried about Claire, just like you're worried about Zahra." Claire had just lost her brother to suicide, and Zahra had recently learned her convicted felon father had been involved in the plot to kill her and Dunphy. The entire team had been on edge until Alex had finally uncovered the mole within the NSA.

Dunphy didn't deny it. Instead he shoved to his feet and stretched, but now that his mischievous itch had been scratched and satisfied for the time being, he was serious again. "And you're worried about Jordyn."

Of course he was. Kickass or not with a weapon, he didn't like her being in danger over here. "Like you're not?"

He shrugged. "Do I wish her, Claire and Zahra were all still stateside with added security? Hell yeah. But they're not, and the truth is with all the shit that's gone down with us all stateside over the past few weeks, they're not facing much more of a threat here than they would be back home by themselves. And the Brits Alex brought on for security are solid. At least we know the girls will be well taken care of while we're out hunting."

Blake hoped so. Although he still thought it odd that Alex would insist Jordyn accompany them to the range yesterday. Had he wanted to see her shoot firsthand? She'd hit pretty much everything, shooting nearly as well as him and Hunter. Unless Alex expected her to go out in the field for some reason? Blake didn't like that thought one bit. He knew Jordyn was good and could take care of herself if necessary, but putting her into harm's way like that wasn't supposed to be part of her job description.

"How's Zahra doing, anyway?" Blake asked to change the subject.

Dunphy climbed into his own bed. "She's tough, man. Way tougher than anyone would ever guess from looking at her. My girl's got a steel backbone inside that delicate frame."

"That's good. Her and Claire work really well together. I'm not surprised Alex wanted to bring them both over here."

"Yeah, those two are a technological powerhouse together."

Gage emerged from the bathroom and stalked past Blake, pausing only to slug Dunphy in the chest on his way back to his bunk. At the muffled oomph and quiet snicker, Blake smiled and closed his eyes. He'd just dropped off to sleep when someone flicked on the lights overhead.

"Wake up, ladies, our ship has just come in."

Rolling over, Blake squinted at Hunter outlined in the doorway.

The team leader was primed and ready to roll. "And it's taking us to Peshawar."

CHAPTER NINE

I t'd been nearly two years since he'd set foot in Peshawar, and it looked like nothing had changed.

Alex strode into the crowded market ahead of Hunter and Blake, who were providing security while Dunphy and Gage stayed in the vehicles. He was comfortable moving on his own in this kind of environment and was more than capable of protecting himself from threats, but having the security team with him meant he could focus almost entirely on the task at hand: finding his informant.

It had taken them two hours to drive here, and even this early in the morning the market was crowded. People filled the walkways between the open stalls crammed with clothing, household items and produce. The cloying smells of spices and body odor hung heavy in the hot, humid air that would only get thicker as the day progressed.

Alex turned sideways to squeeze between a group of men clogging the narrow walkway between two fruit vendors. He didn't have to look to know Hunter and Blake were still behind him, ever watchful and maintaining a careful distance.

The locals stared at him, and not just because he was dressed in a T-shirt and cargo pants instead of the traditional men's shalwar kameez. As westerners—even bearded ones—

they all stood out here, except maybe for Ellis, because he was half black and had a naturally darker skin tone. Alex continued through the maze of stalls and people, intent on the prearranged target near the edge of the market. Like the others, Alex wore an earpiece for communication amongst the team but neither man following him would say anything over it unless a threat materialized.

At the last row of stalls he spotted the man he was supposed to meet. The twenty-one year old Pakistani the NSA had used a couple of times previously for information stood off to the side scanning the crowd, puffing on a cigarette. From his restless movements and the way his gaze kept flitting left then right, Alex knew his informant was a moment from bolting. He could practically feel the man's anxiety from his position forty yards away.

Pushing through the crowd, he kept his eyes on the man. No bulges that might signal a hidden weapon, but it was impossible to be certain with the baggy tunic and pants he wore. When he finally spotted Alex, relief flashed across his face. He came toward Alex and jerked his head to the right, signalling for him to follow. Alex did, knowing his boys were right on his six. At the corner of a brick building the young man stopped and looked around before facing Alex.

"What have you got for me?" Alex asked once the pleasantries were out of the way.

The kid tossed the butt of his cigarette on the ground and crushed it beneath the heel of his leather sandal. "My brother-in-law," he said in accented English.

"What about him?"

"He was working for Hassani."

And the NSA as well. "How do you know this?"

"He told me. There was a meeting last night here in the city."

"What time, and who with?"

"Nine o'clock. And you know who it was with."

That coincided perfectly with the subsequent phone call they'd managed to trace back to a number linked to one of Hassani's men at just after twenty-one-thirty hours last night. "Do you know what happened at the meeting?"

The man shook his head, running the back of his hand under his upper lip. There was fear in his eyes. "No one has seen him. His wife said he left at eight-thirty and didn't return home last night. It's not like him, he always comes home."

Alex didn't need to tell the guy that his brother-in-law was either long dead or wishing he was. Hassani had evidently found out about the man's involvement with the NSA and had taken precautions to eliminate the threat. "What else do you know?"

"There was a car." He licked his lips, gaze darting around the people milling past them before coming to rest on Alex once again. "Someone reported witnessing a scuffle between two big, armed men and another unarmed one last night in the area where the meeting was supposed to have happened, around the same time. My brother-in-law would never willingly get into a car with those kind of men. They headed west out of the city, toward the border." He swallowed. "I went to the house when I got the call from my…friend about the incident. Another vehicle left twenty minutes later and took the same route. I followed them to the border and watched them drive across."

Alex's heart beat faster. His attention sharpened on the young guy, everything else funneling out. "Did you get the plate number?"

"Yes, of course." He reached into his pocket and pulled out a folded piece of paper, handed it to him. "I didn't see who was inside and the windows were too dark for me to see how many people were in there, but...I think it must have been Hassani."

Alex sure as hell hoped it was. As soon as he got Claire and Zahra to run the plate number, they could potentially get satellite or drone images from last night, or at least start a search now. Still, he played it cool, keeping his expression passive. "Anything else?"

The man shook his head. "My brother-in-law... Is he dead?"

"Most likely."

He lowered his eyes and nodded, face pinched with grief.

"I'll be in touch if I need anything else. You might want to lie low for a while though." Alex reached out a hand. When the man shook it, Alex passed him the wad of US cash he'd been palming, then turned and quickly headed back through the market, taking a different route this time. He didn't see Hunter or Ellis but he knew they were still out there keeping tabs on him.

Pulling out his phone, he called Claire and gave her the information to start tracking the plate and checking satellite feeds. Near the main street he turned right and headed for the alley where the SUVs were waiting. He was just about to turn the corner when out of his peripheral vision he caught a flash of auburn hair beneath a deep purple head scarf. He whipped his head around and stopped so fast he almost stumbled.

In a group of people crowded around a vendor, a woman stood with her back to him. At this distance he couldn't see her face, but that glimpse of red hair he'd seen, the stance and the way she moved her hands when she talked...

Grace?

Impossible.

Pulse thudding in his ears, his heart careened wildly in his chest. Everything else fell away, his entire focus zeroing in on that figure in the crowd. Without even realizing he'd moved, he was jogging toward her.

"Alex, what the hell's going on?" Hunter demanded in his ear.

He ignored the question, intent only on reaching the woman before she disappeared. The hope and desperation inside him were crushing his lungs, making it hard to breathe. Running now, he tore back across the road and pushed his way through the throng of people separating him from the woman. Just when he was starting to gain ground the crowd shifted and the woman was gone. Swearing silently, he jerked to a halt and scanned the market.

The sea of bodies swirled and eddied. In a gap in the distance he spotted the purple head scarf, the flash of red hair beneath it. Her name swelled in his throat, his brain demanding he shout it out, make her turn around. But it was already too late. She was lost in the crowd.

At the sound of running footsteps behind him he whirled around. Hunter stopped beside him, gaze scanning for threats, a scowl on his hard face. Finding nothing, he turned on Alex with a fierce glower. "What the hell was that about? We thought you were chasing a tango."

"Nothing. Forget it." Now that he'd been snapped out of whatever the hell state he'd just been in, he realized people were staring at the both of them. Not good, and especially not here and now when a terrorist network was trying to hunt them all down and kill them.

Alex mentally shook himself. He'd lost his fucking mind, thinking he'd seen Grace here after all this time. That was the only explanation. Last he'd heard, she'd taken a job in London with a humanitarian group a few months back. Maybe it wasn't healthy or even ethical, but he'd kept partial tabs on her over the past four years, telling himself it was only to make sure she was doing okay after what she'd been through. After all, he was largely responsible for what she'd suffered. Little wonder she hadn't returned any of his calls or tried to look him up after she separated from her husband.

Hunter eyed him skeptically. "You sure you're good?"

He'd just hallucinated about seeing a woman he hadn't seen or spoken to in over four years, then run blindly through a crowded market known to be frequented by members of the very cell he was trying to kill, with no regard for his own safety or for that of the team, let alone a thought to compromising the mission. Jesus. He really was losing it. "Yeah. Let's get back to the trucks. Where's Ellis?"

"Providing overwatch, because we thought you were about to get into the shit," he muttered, turning and striding away.

Berating himself for his kneejerk and reckless—not to mention fucking stupid and flat out dangerous—reaction, he followed Hunter back to the vehicles. Ellis fell in step with them, eyeing him in confusion. "What happened?"

"Nothing," Alex snapped. He could see the vehicles, one parked behind the other, Gage behind the wheel of the first and Dunphy's silhouette in the second. No doubt they'd heard the whole embarrassing incident too. Thankfully he was saved from any more questions by the vibration of his phone against his hip. It was Claire.

Anticipation stirred inside him. "Hey. Whatcha got?"

"The plates didn't give us anything except that the vehicle definitely crossed the border last night at twenty-two-eleven, zulu."

Eleven minutes after ten, local time. It fit with what the informant had said. "And the occupants?"

"Two men, but only one produced documents to the border guard. We've traced the vehicle via satellite to the

Khyber Pass, but at the first checkpoint the authorities claim only the driver was in the car."

He was ninety percent sure it had been Hassani in that backseat. And he was just as certain that their number one high value target was making cozy with the locals in the mountains of eastern Afghanistan right now. "Roger that. Have Evers and his guys meet us at the place we arranged, STAT. I'll brief you again from the other side." He hung up and walked around the hood of the SUV to slide in beside Gage, tapping his earpiece. "Saddle up boys, we're headed across the border."

It felt good to be on the move and finally across the border into Afghanistan, even if they were now traveling through the infamous Khyber Pass in the Spin Ghar Mountains. Blake sat in the back of the SUV. So far the traffic was relatively light, only a few minibuses loaded with civilians and the odd military vehicle carrying supplies toward Kabul. Everyone was quiet in the truck. Gage was focused on the winding road, Alex was talking and texting on his phone and Blake kept an eye out for any trouble.

It had been an interesting morning so far, that was for sure.

Blake wasn't sure what the hell had happened back in that Peshawar market, but Alex had taken off after someone and then just as suddenly stopped. At first Blake had thought he'd seen Hassani, or at least someone from his network, but now he wasn't so sure. Hunter'd been pissed that he'd raced off and broken radio communication without telling them what the hell was going on. The place had been crowded and filled with all kinds of potential threats, including lots of shadowy hiding spots if anyone was inclined to take a rifle and do some hunting from one of the windows of the buildings surrounding the square.

Now that they were away from that mass of bodies and on the road, Blake felt a lot more relaxed. He was in the lead vehicle with Gage and Alex this time, while Hunter drove Evers and another Fed in the second and Dunphy brought up the rear with two more of Evers's boys. They'd left another SUV back at HQ for the Brits and the girls. The plan was to pick up the trail where Hassani had left the highway last night. But in order to do that, they still needed one more solid piece of human intel or a clue from a passing satellite to give them a direction.

Alex's phone beeped with another incoming message. He glanced down at it and relayed the info to him and Gage. "Zahra's translated some recent chatter we found. There's a meeting between a few Taliban leaders in a village happening this morning, and this transmission was pinged at seventy-five miles southeast of Jalalabad. Apparently they're expecting an important guest they've named 'The Scorpion'."

"Sounds promising," Gage muttered.

"Any satellite images in the area?" Blake asked.

Alex typed something into his phone. "She and Claire are working on that now." Then he tapped his earpiece and brought the others up to speed.

Blake leaned over to peer between the front seats and check the dashboard. The on-screen GPS showed another narrowing in the road coming up. This one had a hairpin turn, and judging by the steeply sloping terrain, it was right next to a canyon.

Gage slowed down to make the upcoming turn easier, and also to let the other vehicles stack up closer behind them. Going by the map this was the most likely spot for an ambush that Blake could see, so it made sense to keep them grouped tight together and therefore pose a more formidable and tougher target.

Gage made the turn and picked up speed despite the way the road narrowed. About a mile up ahead around the end of the hairpin Blake could see the minibus easing out of the curve. There were no vehicles coming at them the other way, and the closest one to them was about a half mile behind. He breathed a little easier at not being boxed in at the upcoming turn.

Blake braced a hand on the doorframe as Gage took the first part of the hairpin at an aggressive speed. The big vehicle's tires slid slightly but Gage corrected with ease and didn't let up on the gas. Up ahead around the tight curve at the end, the road was still empty. Hunter's vehicle was right on their six, and Dunphy in formation after him.

Gage eased out of the turn and hit the gas. The SUV shot forward—

An explosion boomed behind them.

Shit!

Blake and Alex whipped around in their seats as the concussion reverberated through the SUV. The pressure wave hit Blake in the chest and pushed against his eardrums. Gage stomped on the gas harder and as soon as they were out of the turn, pulled up short in a screeching skid at the side of the road. Through the back window Blake saw the flash of orange and a cloud of black smoke rising up from the last vehicle.

"It's Dunphy," he reported, adrenaline blasting through him as they all grabbed for their weapons and leapt out of the vehicle.

"Get the med kit," Alex barked at Gage, then ran with Blake toward the burning vehicle. Hunter and the others from his vehicle were already out and fanning around the last SUV.

A roadside bomb had ripped into the undercarriage, igniting the fuel, and no one had gotten out yet.

Shoving his pistol back into its holster, Blake ran to help get the passengers out. Hunter had already reached in and wrenched the driver's door open when Blake got there. Behind the wheel Dunphy was conscious but not really alert, moaning and not moving as they unhooked the seatbelt and dragged him out. Whatever damage they caused by moving him was secondary to losing him to the fire. Evers and Gage were attempting to pull the others from the wreckage as Alex sprayed the flames with a fire extinguisher.

Even as he hauled his buddy out of the wreckage, Blake cast a furtive glance around him. Were there shooters up there, ready to attack? Nothing caught his eye.

He and Hunter rushed Dunphy back to the first vehicle and laid him down on a blanket someone had spread beside the SUV in a sheltered spot between the vehicle and the hillside. Immediately they got to work checking his airway and doing an initial assessment. Dunphy was breathing on his own and his eyes were open, but he wasn't moving and both his legs were chewed up and bleeding like hell from the shrapnel wounds he'd sustained.

Blake supported his neck in case there was a spinal injury and leaned over to look into those dark, glazed eyes. "Say something, man," he ordered him, his guts knotted tight at seeing his friend and spotter lying so still and bloody.

"Bomb," Dunphy mumbled. Gage was cutting away the ruined pant legs to get a better look at the damage that went all the way up to Dunphy's thighs.

"Yeah, your truck got hit. Can you move your arms and legs?"

He was already pale, but at that he blanched beneath his growth of black facial hair. Beads of sweat popped out across his skin. "Can't feel my legs."

Blake shoved down the leap of fear that shot up his own spine. "It's okay, man, you're in shock. Just take it easy and slow your heart rate down. Gage and I've got you."

Dunphy tried to lift his head, eyes wide as he looked down the length of his body and saw all the blood. "Can't fucking feel my *legs*," he bit out, the words laced with terror.

"They're still there," Gage assured him, applying pressure dressings to both limbs. "You're bleeding all over though, so lie still and get that heart rate down. Understand?"

Dunphy dropped his head back into Blake's hands and squeezed his eyes shut. "Oh, Jesus Christ…"

"It'll be okay, man," Blake insisted, not caring if it was a lie at this point. They needed Dunphy to calm down or he risked bleeding out before they could get him to a hospital.

Alex ran back to them, already on his satellite phone as Gage started an IV in Dunphy's arm. Alex was giving coordinates and a nine line to whoever was on the end, and Blake guessed it must be some sort of military medevac unit. "Two KIA and one other severely wounded," he said to them after he'd ended the call. He knelt beside Dunphy and set a firm hand on the guy's shoulder. "Helo's inbound from Bagram, ETA thirty-five minutes."

Dunphy merely nodded, eyes screwed shut and his teeth bared. He might not be feeling his legs, but he was feeling a shitload of pain elsewhere. Alex left to continue coordinating the rescue. Blake reached one hand down to put pressure on one of the worst wounds in his friend's lower leg to help slow the bleeding.

A minute later Hunter appeared and dropped to his knees beside Dunphy. "What do you need?"

"Zahra," came the raspy answer. "Somebody call Zahra."

Blake exchanged looks with Hunter and Gage. When they both hesitated, Blake stepped in. "I'll do it. Hold his head steady," he said to Hunter, exchanging places with him. He walked away out of earshot before dialing Jordyn's cell. All the while he kept careful watch of the surrounding hills and road, but traffic had stopped in both directions and none of the onlookers approached them. The hills remained empty. Whoever had set off the bomb had detonated it remotely and run away like the cowardly fuckers they were.

Jordyn answered on the third ring, her voice bright and cheerful. "Hello, handsome. I was just thinking about you."

"Hey." His voice nearly cracked on the single word.

"What's wrong?" she demanded.

"IED. Dunphy's truck got hit."

"Oh my God, is he all right?"

He had to swallow past the lump in his throat before continuing. "No, but he's alive." *For now, at least.* "Two others in his vehicle are dead and one more wounded. Medevac chopper's on its way, should be here in the next half hour."

"How bad is he?" He could hear the tension and worry in her voice.

"He says he can't feel his legs." Her sharply indrawn breath echoed exactly how he was feeling. Angry, horrified and helpless, not a comfortable mix for someone used to taking action and being in control. "They're still attached but they're all torn up and he's bleeding bad. I dunno…"

"Blake, I'm so sorry. Is there anything I can do?"

He sucked in a steadying breath before answering. "I need you to tell Zahra."

She hesitated only a moment. "Okay."

"Just tell her there was an accident and that he's okay. Let her know about the medevac. Don't tell her about his legs.

Make it clear he's conscious and alert right now and we're taking care of him. Then call me back once she's calm. He wants to talk to her." To hear her voice and draw on that as his anchor. Fuck, he was going to start bawling.

"I'm on it. She'll call you back ASAP."

"Thanks."

"Blake? I love you."

He closed his eyes, fighting the sting of tears. God, until this moment he hadn't realized just how much he'd been dreaming of hearing those words from her. Her saying them now almost snapped his tenuous hold on his composure, because he knew why she was telling him now over the phone. Because anything could happen to any of them, at any time. Dunphy getting hit was a stark reminder that Blake might never get the chance to tell Jordyn how he truly felt if he didn't say it now.

His deeply buried fear of rejection could go fuck itself. He needed her to know what she meant to him. "Love you too," he said in a rough voice. The words seemed so inadequate but they were all he had and he'd never meant anything more. "Bye."

Hanging up, he hurried back to Dunphy. His buddy was still alert but shaking all over now despite the heat and the blanket someone had draped over him. Gage was in the middle of applying new dressings to replace the saturated ones. Blake had seen a lot of blood during his tour overseas, but seeing it coming out of one of his buddies would never get any easier.

He knelt at Dunphy's shoulder and met that fear-filled gaze squarely. "Zahra's gonna call you in just a minute, okay?"

The spotter nodded, mouth pinched. "Tell her I'm okay," he blurted.

"You can tell her yourself when she calls. Jordyn's alerting her right now."

A tight, jerky nod. "If I pass out, or don't…tell her I love her."

Fuck. Blake fought back the sickening pang of dread that ricocheted in his chest. "You'll say it yourself, brother. Just relax and hang in there." Not knowing what else to do, he reached beneath the blanket to find Dunphy's hand and gripped it tight, relieved when those ice cold fingers squeezed back.

A few minutes later his phone rang. He answered, instantly recognizing Zahra's frantic voice. "He's holding his own," Blake said to reassure her. "He just needs to hear your voice right now, okay? You gotta stay calm, Zahra. We're taking care of him and will get him to a hospital as soon as that chopper shows up. I'll be right next to him the whole time." He hadn't asked Alex or Hunter permission for that, but he didn't really care if they liked it or not. There was no way he was leaving Dunphy's side until the medical staff took over at the hospital.

"Let me talk to him," she pleaded, the tears in her voice shredding him as she struggled to calm down.

"Okay, here he is." He put the phone to Dunphy's ear. It felt like an anvil was pressing on his chest as he watched his buddy visibly relax at the sound of her voice. The blanket and road beneath his lower body was stained with his blood. Blake could smell the cloying, iron-tinged smell of it in the hot air.

"Hey, sweetness," Dunphy managed between chattering teeth. "I love you."

Blake swallowed and looked away, glad he'd had the sense to tell Jordyn that a few minutes ago.

Unable to give them any privacy, he held the phone for his friend and stayed where he was. Blake knelt there in the dust at the side of the road and maintained his grip on that cold hand. He prayed silently and repeatedly until he finally heard the muted whump of rotors in the distance.

CHAPTER TEN

When the door to the Islamabad hospital waiting room finally opened and Blake walked through it, Jordyn's heart lurched at the sight of him. He had bloodstains on his shirt and pants and the emotional toll of everything was there in his eyes. Exhaustion. Anger. Helplessness. Worry.

Immediately she jumped up, walked over to him and wrapped her arms around his wide back, holding on tight. Rather than remain stiff or step away as she'd partly expected, he returned the embrace and rested his cheek against the top of her head. A hard sigh escaped him. After a moment he squeezed her once and let go, putting some space between them. "Thanks for coming."

She sought his gaze and read the weariness there, along with everything he was trying to lock away. "Of course. How is he?"

"In surgery." His tone was flat, tired.

"Where's Zahra?"

"Talking with a couple of the doctors. She's doing as well as can be expected. Tom's going to stay the night with her here, then at least until tomorrow afternoon."

Jordyn relaxed a bit. Zahra had been understandably upset on the drive over with her and Lang. The other Brit, Wright, was back at HQ with Claire. Jordyn had done what she could to comfort Zahra during the past few hours, but really, there was nothing she could say or do to make any of this easier. Knowing the man you loved had been severely wounded, that the extent of the injuries was uncertain and there was fuck-all you could do to help him? That was the stuff of nightmares. "What's the prognosis, do you know?"

Blake pushed out a breath and scrubbed a hand over his closely shorn hair before answering. He'd known Dunphy for a lot longer than she had, so she knew what a blow this was for him. "Both femurs fractured, and the bones in his lower legs as well. Some arterial bleeding, too. The orthopedic surgeon said he can fix all that, so unless they find something unexpected when they go in, at this point there's no worry he'll lose his legs."

God. "And what about…" She couldn't say it.

He shook his head tightly. For a split second his expression became full of torment, cracking the calm facade he was trying his damnedest to hide behind. "No sensation at all from the waist down. They said his spinal cord's intact but there's so much swelling from the blast that they can't tell the extent of the damage yet, or whether it's permanent or not. We won't know for at least a few days, maybe more."

If Dunphy would ever walk again, he meant.

She'd been expecting that while hoping for the best, but hearing the awful possibility out loud made tears clog her throat. She just couldn't imagine charming, fun-loving and devilish Sean Dunphy confined to a wheelchair for the rest of his days.

"Ah, hell, I know," Blake murmured, drawing her into the safety of his embrace once again. She shut her eyes and held onto him, trying to get a grip on herself. Crying her eyes out wouldn't change anything, and Blake was upset enough, no matter how calm and strong he was trying to be. "He's a fighter, angel. He'll give it everything he has."

She nodded, letting the endearment and the deep rumble of his voice wash over her like a balm. Blake was right, she knew he was, but this broke her heart. And she kept thinking that it could've been him on that operating table right now, her in Zahra's place. She clutched at the back of his blood-stained T-shirt and drew a few deep, steadying breaths. When she was sure she had control again she gently pushed away and wiped at her eyes with the heels of her hands. "What do we need to do now?"

A hint of a smile curved his mouth and she saw the admiration in his gaze at her changing the subject. He opened his mouth, closed it, and she knew he was choosing his words with care. When he spoke his voice was low and serious. "What we said on the phone?"

Her face heated, but she forced herself to hold his gaze. Was he going to take it back? Retreat emotionally from her now because he'd merely said it in the heat of the moment? Because she refused to let him. "I meant it."

He nodded. His eyes shifted to his hand as he reached up to tuck a lock of hair behind her ear. "I meant it too. I'm just not used to saying it to anyone outside my family, so I'm a little rusty."

The unspoken apology in his words made her heart squeeze. "You just need practice, that's all."

He met her gaze. The look in his eyes changed, heated. The territorial light she saw burning there thrilled her. She didn't need to hear the words again from him right now— yeah, they'd be nice, but she knew he loved her and she was willing to let him get comfortable with the idea on his own terms. Things had changed so fast between them. She was secure in his feelings for her and wanted to make sure she was there for him, helped support him however she could through this.

He opened his mouth to say something else but the door opened and Tom walked in. The stocky former SEAL gave her a weary smile and ran a hand over his short brown hair before turning his attention on Blake. "Nothing else you guys can do for now, and Alex will want you back in the field soon. Both of you go back to HQ and get cleaned up, get some rest if you can."

"You sure?" Blake asked, clearly hesitant. "I'd feel better waiting until he's out of the O.R. at least."

"Like I said, there's nothing more you can do here. I'll update you as soon as I know anything."

"What about Zahra?" Jordyn asked. "I can stay with her." And Zahra might be more comfortable with her staying here, another female, rather than Tom.

The Titanium chief shook his head. "You're probably going to have to help Claire out for a while. Evers is still with the rest of the guys and Zahra won't be up to working right now so she's gonna need help. Things are gonna start moving fast from here on in. Everyone's itching to find out who pulled this stunt today, and hit them hard once we do."

Jordyn understood that, but she hadn't thought she'd wind up working on Claire's side of things. She was a decent mechanic and handy with a long gun. She wasn't a computer wizard.

"Go on," Tom insisted, waving them away. "I've already contacted Dunphy's family and the insurance people have things rolling. Everything's under control. I've got the situation covered."

Jordyn looked at Blake for confirmation. She realized there was nothing they could actually do, but she still felt guilty for leaving Sean and Zahra like this.

Blake gave her his answer by setting an arm around her shoulders and tugging her toward the door. "Come on, let's go."

Lang was waiting out in the SUV and drove them back across town to HQ. Blake was up front, her in the back, and no one talked during the twenty-five minute drive. By the time they arrived at the concrete building currently serving as home, Blake had retreated into himself. She knew the signs because she'd seen them all before when Jamie died. He was quiet and tense, lost in his own head, and she didn't know how to pull him back out again. Or if she even should. Everyone dealt with grief differently.

Once inside, Blake muttered something to her about cleaning up and headed into the barracks. Lang went back outside to join Wright, so Jordyn went to see if she could help Claire.

The blonde cryptologist stood when she saw her. Her gentle gray eyes were puffy and red as if she'd been crying a lot. "How is he?"

"Should be out of surgery soon, but we won't know about the spinal injuries for a while at least."

Claire nodded and lowered her gaze to the floor. She chewed on her bottom lip, seemed to be struggling to maintain her composure. At last she looked up at Jordyn again. "Gage was almost killed not long ago on another op with the team."

She hid a wince, didn't say that she already knew about the incident. "I'm sorry." This had to be bringing up all kinds of demons for her. God knew it was making Jordyn even more afraid for Blake.

Claire drew in a breath and wiped at her face. "He said he'd be phasing out of field work after this. I just pray he…" She trailed off and shook her head, clearly unable to finish that thought. "God, poor Zahra."

"Tom's with her." That sounded so stupid and lame, but it was all she could say to reassure her. "He told me to check in with you and see if I could give you a hand with anything."

Claire's face brightened. "Yes! God, yes. More intel comes in every minute, I swear." She reached out, grabbed Jordyn by the hand and dragged her over to Zahra's open laptop, still sitting on the table. "Know anything about accessing satellite feeds?"

"Uh, no. You're gonna have to walk me through everything. And use small words while you do, okay?"

Claire let out a quiet laugh as Jordyn sank into Zahra's chair. "Okay, no problem. It's not that hard once you get the hang of it."

Jordyn did her best to keep up and follow instructions. Claire's fingers flew across the keyboard at lightning speed. Soon some aerial shots of the region they were interested in showed up on screen.

"There's the village Alex flagged for us earlier," Claire told her, pointing to the group of dun-colored mud brick buildings in the center of the shot. "There've been men coming and going from there for a few hours now. Here are the close-ups. See if you can find any matches in this facial recognition database." She brought up another screen, her fingers a blur on the keys. Jordyn was utterly lost.

"What's the latest?"

She breathed out an audible sigh of relief at that deep voice coming from the doorway. Blake crossed the room to stand behind Jordyn's seat. She was acutely aware of the way he leaned over her, his muscled arms braced on either side of her chair. The clean scent of soap and shampoo surrounded her, telling her he'd just taken a shower in the one tiny cubicle they had.

"We're trying to pair the men at the meeting in the village with matches from NSAnet," Claire told him, still focused on the screen as she typed in more commands, brought up the other program and entered her username and password. "Alex and the others are headed toward this location now. They're hoping we'll get a hit to confirm this is the right target before they head out from their current position on foot."

Jordyn glanced up at Blake's strong profile as he studied the terrain with expert eyes. "What's their position now?" he asked.

Claire sighed, her frown broadcasting her worry. "About six miles southwest, last I heard." More typing, and a satellite map popped up on screen. "Here," she said, pointing. "That's their last known position."

Only a few miles from the road where Dunphy had been hit, by the looks of it. "They're moving in there in broad daylight?" Jordyn asked, shocked by the very idea. Why would Alex risk it, especially after they'd just lost Dunphy and his passengers to an enemy attack?

Blake made a negative sound. "Just getting into a good observation position. Once they confirm the target, they'll move as soon as it's dark."

Claire's phone pinged. She grabbed it from the table, read the message and looked up at Blake. Her gray eyes were wide, anxious. "It's Alex. He wants you out there ASAP and asked you to bring more weapons and ammo."

Because a lot of it had been destroyed when Dunphy's SUV was hit, and without the wounded and Blake the team was suddenly down to four guys instead of eight. She hated the thought of him going out there, being outnumbered and exposed in enemy territory. A lead weight settled in the pit of Jordyn's stomach. Her fingers tightened around the mouse.

Blake set a hand on her shoulder, squeezed gently. "Help me get everything ready?"

"Sure." She pushed the chair back and rose to follow him downstairs.

The large walk-in storage closet they'd turned into a loadout room was at the end of the garage where she'd been working. Jordyn flipped on the light, stepped into the room with Blake right on her heels and immediately went to the wall of lockers at the opposite end. Opening one, she reached for the boxes of ammo on the top shelf. The sound of the dead bolt sliding home behind her startled her.

She turned. "What—" The words died in her throat.

Blake stood with his back to the door. He was staring right at her with such an intense, hungry expression that the air locked in her lungs.

The sudden rise of pressure in her chest cavity kicked her heart into high gear. She couldn't move, could only stare back at him as arousal pulsed through her body. Jordyn licked her lips. With him facing uncertainty in the field for God knew how long and the intensity of the current situation facing the team, they both needed this. Need roared through her, hot and urgent.

Blake's nostrils flared in response, his eyes all hot and molten. His gaze raked over her like he wanted to devour her. Jordyn was more than willing to be his prey.

She blindly set the box of ammo back on the shelf.

Before she could take a single step, Blake erased the small distance between them, took her face in his hands and brought his mouth down on hers in a voracious kiss. Urgent, desperate. Her gasp was lost in his mouth as his tongue drove between her lips to taste her. She grabbed hold of his hard biceps and gave as good as she got, meeting every stroke of his tongue with frantic need.

Blake made a low, rough sound of approval in the back of his throat and gripped her hips. He hauled her up and drove her backward until her shoulder blades hit the wall. Her legs automatically wound around his waist, bringing the ache between her thighs in direct contact with the rigid length of his erection. A soft cry spilled free at the feel of him, so hot and hungry against her. Blake's hold tightened on her hips as he kissed her senseless and rubbed himself against her in slow, delicious circles that lit every nerve ending in her body on fire.

Her nipples were beaded into tight points against the cotton of her sports bra. She rubbed against him like an animal in heat, desperate for more friction. For whatever he would give her. She'd been longing for this for so long and now she finally had the chance to show just how much she loved and wanted him. She didn't care that it was happening in a storage closet, only that she was going to have him inside her soon.

His lips broke away from hers to blaze a fiery path down her neck. He found that sensitive spot where it curved into her shoulder and licked at it, scraping the very edge of his teeth against her skin. Jordyn gasped as she threw her head back to give him better access and rubbed the hot glow between her thighs against him. She was reeling, so wet already, her body empty and aching for him.

One strong hand left her hip to shove at the hem of her T-shirt. She helped him peel it over her head and tossed it aside, shivering in anticipation when those gold-flecked eyes locked on the outline of her nipples visible through her bra. Without hesitation he grabbed the bottom of it and yanked upward, tugging the fabric up and off as she raised her arms.

Cool air washed over her heated skin, making the sensitive points throb unbearably. Blake let out a low, possessive growl then bent to take a nipple in his mouth. Streaks of lightning shot through her from where his lips and tongue tormented her, arrowing down to where he rubbed against her needy flesh so seductively.

On fire and uncaring about anything other than assuaging the terrible ache inside her, she grabbed hold of the back of his head to hold him where he was and arched her back, demanding more. Pleasure swelled and twisted inside her, a hot, unbearable throbbing that only he could ease. He nipped at her tender flesh before switching to the other nipple, driving the heat higher until she was panting, writhing, rubbing wantonly against his hard body. The teasing friction wasn't nearly enough. She needed him inside her, filling and claiming her completely.

Without warning he released her breast, set her on her feet and spun her around to face the waist high cabinet set against the opposite wall. She barely had time to throw her hands out to catch herself before he was on her again, this time pressing one hand between her shoulder blades as he pulled her hips back with the other. His arm locked around her hips. Mind spinning, muscles shaking, Jordyn didn't even think of protesting. The raw urgency in his hold only pushed her arousal higher. She bent forward and let the cabinet support her, the cool metal surface chilly against her nipples.

"A bed next time, Jordyn," he rasped against her ear, stirring goosebumps. "So I can lay you down and do this right."

She heard the apology in his voice, but this felt pretty goddamn right to her, and she loved that he was already thinking of the next time. "It's okay," she whispered, needing him to believe her. If this fast fuck against a cabinet was all she could have of him for now, she'd take it.

Blake's hands shot to the front of her pants. He yanked the zipper down and shoved them halfway down her thighs.

Jordyn stayed still. He made a low sound of approval at the sight she presented. Jordyn all but purred as he smoothed a hand down her spine, over the curve of her ass, then swept her white cotton boy shorts down with one tug.

Bent over with her most intimate parts on display for him, she didn't move, every muscle quivering with anticipation. Warm, long fingers traced over the curve of her butt then down the sensitive back of one thigh before dipping between her legs where she was hot and melting for him. Her head snapped up, a muffled moan tearing free as he penetrated her with a finger. He hissed in a breath when he felt how wet she was, then his hand withdrew and she heard the unmistakable sound of a foil wrapper tearing.

God, yes, she urged him, swinging her head around to watch. The sight of him shot her arousal even higher. Fully clothed except where he'd opened his pants to free his erection, he was a sight to behold. He slid the condom over the thick, hard length standing so proudly away from his body, then lifted his gaze and locked it on her. The naked possessiveness and need she read there turned her to mush and revved her higher at the same time.

He reached forward to grip her hands and wrap them around the edge of the cabinet. "Hold on," he rasped against her cheek, a command and erotic warning rolled into one.

She shivered at the dark note of hunger in his voice, her body tightening, dying for that moment when he finally drove into her. Her fingers curled around that cool metal until the knuckles turned white and she sought his mouth when he eased his upper body back.

Blake wrapped one hand around her right hip and reached up to fist the other in her hair, twisting her face up to his. His kiss was wild and desperate, matching the unrelieved pressure inside her. He pulled her hips toward him and she felt the blunt head of his cock at her entrance. Hard. Hot. Still kissing him, she tried to push back toward him more but he held her firm and slid forward in a hard, deep thrust.

Jordyn cried out, the sound drowned in his mouth as her body squeezed around the thick length inside her. She was still adjusting to the size of him, processing the sheer sensation of him stretching her when he slid a hand around to cup her mound and rubbed a finger against the aching bud of her clit. Her knees wobbled. A high, strained sound clawed its way out of her throat before she could stop it.

Blake hummed in approval. He nipped at her lower lip then soothed the sting with the caress of his tongue before breaking the kiss. She could feel the tension in him, those powerful muscles quivering as he held back. They were both panting, straining, the air infused with the scent of soap and perspiration and sex. Still stroking her most sensitive spot with his fingers, he withdrew his cock slightly and eased forward again, his attention riveted to her face to observe her reaction.

Spots danced in front of her eyes when he hit that perfect place inside her. Her head fell forward, suddenly too heavy for her to hold up. "God, Blake…"

With a deep, pleased purr he repeated the movement, sliding over that incredibly sensitive spot inside her as he caressed her clit and placed hot, open-mouth kisses down her neck. The swelling pleasure suddenly intensified, her body reaching greedily for the orgasm building deep in her core. She'd waited so long for this, had yearned for it for *years*. The teasing was killing her. She needed him faster, deeper, harder. Right. Fucking. Now.

With an almost feral snarl she reached back to dig her fingers into his ass and reared her hips back. He growled against her neck and tightened his hold on her hip, stilling her effortlessly with controlled strength. Ignoring her protesting whimper, he began easing the head of his cock in and out of her in a slow, devastating rhythm that had her whole body quaking.

"*Blake.*" She couldn't stand this. Couldn't take the exquisite torture.

He continued with the slow in and out glide as though he wanted to savor every moment, sliding over that internal hot spot with each motion of his hips. The soft, slick sounds of him stroking in and out of her were the most erotic thing she'd ever heard. And when he punctuated them with low, nearly inaudible groans that vibrated in his chest and told her just how agonizingly good it was for him too, the first tremors of impending release hit her.

Blake let go of her hip to reach up and turn her face toward him again. Jordyn forced her heavy lids apart. His expression was intent, focused, so full of heat she should have combusted on the spot. "Need to see your face when you come for me," he gritted out.

The words, the sheer possessiveness behind them, pushed her to the precipice of that towering cliff. Helpless in the grip of the most powerful pleasure she'd ever known, Jordyn lost the battle to keep her eyes open. Blake's mouth was there to capture her cry of surrender, hot and damp against her lips, her neck. "Jordyn. My Jordyn," he muttered.

The finger between her legs pressed harder as he finally sped up his thrusts, and everything inside her clenched tight. She let the wave take her, crying out her pleasure into his mouth as he caught her lips beneath his and rode her through her orgasm. It blasted through her in a series of shockwaves that went right to her toes before eventually softening into ripples.

Boneless, gasping, she tore her mouth free from his and slumped forward. With her hot, damp cheek resting on top of the cabinet, she felt him drive deep and stiffen, every muscle pressed against her rigid as his own release hit. His tormented groan filled the small space.

She had no idea how much time passed before he curved over her limp body to nuzzle her neck and press a soft, lingering kiss to the corner of her mouth. His tongue eased across her lower lip in a tender caress, as though he couldn't stop tasting her. At last he eased up and back, bathing her spine and hips in a cool wash of air as he withdrew and pulled his pants up.

She'd just found the strength to get her arms beneath her and push her torso up from the cabinet when he caught her around the waist and raised her with nothing but the strength of his arm. God that was sexy, knowing he could overpower her if he chose but only using that strength to cherish her.

He helped her get her pants back up, then turned her around and enveloped her in a protective embrace. Holding her tight he sank to the floor where she straddled his thighs as he cradled her, one hand cupping the back of her head.

Still floating, she moaned a protest when he eased her away from his body and stood, pulling her to her feet with him. He tugged her bra and shirt over her head. She blinked up into his handsome face as she made herself presentable, amazed by the love shining in his eyes. He let her see it, held nothing back as he ran a thumb across her cheek. "You all right?"

Was he kidding? The man had reduced her to a puddle of bliss and she still couldn't speak. She nodded instead.

His eyes glowed with tenderness, his expression full of regret. "I hate leaving like this, but I've gotta get moving. Let's get what we came in here for, huh?"

What? Oh, the ammo.

They came out with two packed duffels a few minutes later and headed back up to see Claire, Jordyn's thighs trembling slightly with each step. Blake had literally left her weak in the knees. If Claire knew what they'd been doing when she saw them she didn't let on, and instead handed her phone to Blake. "Alex just called me. Wants to talk to you."

Blake pulled out his own phone. He dialed, spoke to Alex briefly, then his eyes shot to her. Jordyn swallowed at the shock she saw written there, and braced for more bad news as Blake ended the call and stared at her.

"What?" she whispered. Was it Dunphy?

"Alex wants me to link up with the ground team by nightfall, and he wants me to bring you along. Apparently you're my new spotter."

CHAPTER ELEVEN

S ean dragged his strangely weighted eyelids open and struggled to focus on his surroundings. The light was too low for him to see anything at first. His mouth was dry and he was groggy as shit, like he'd been drugged or something. Wherever he was it was dim and smelled slightly stale, the air overlaid with the sharp sting of antiseptic.

As his eyes slowly focused on his surroundings he became aware of faint, shuffling footsteps beyond the room he was in, and the pain radiating up his back and arms. He blinked, made out the shape of the small rectangular room, then saw the rails on either side of him and realized he was lying in a hospital bed.

In an instant, everything slammed front and center into his brain. The winding Khyber Pass, the explosion, coming to as someone hauled him from the burning wreckage. Trying to scream and not being able to. Regaining consciousness again later to see Gage's frantic attempt to stop the bleeding in his legs—

His *legs*.

He shot up on his elbows and craned his neck down the length of his supine body to get a better look. He could see the outline of them beneath the blankets, but he couldn't feel them so he blinked again, praying he wasn't imagining things. Cold sweat popped out on his face and chest. Maybe the doctors had frozen him during the surgery. It looked like there were two long lumps beneath the covers down there.

"They're still there."

His head snapped around at the sound of that soft, familiar voice. Zahra was walking toward him from where a chair sat next to the window. His heart clenched in terror at the tear stains on her cheeks, the sorrow in her wet, puffy eyes. Zahra was one of the strongest people he knew and she didn't cry easily, but clearly she'd been bawling for a while. His pulse echoed in his ears. Oh, shit, he didn't think he could bear it but he had to know.

He reached out blindly for her hand, relieved beyond measure when she gripped his tight and brought it to her damp cheek. The panic was clawing at him, threatening to close his throat off. "What happened? What did the doctors say?" He was panting, his body reacting to the fear with a surge of adrenaline.

Zahra pressed her lips together and looked up at the ceiling, blinking rapidly for a few seconds before she found her composure and met his gaze once more. "They stopped the bleeding and fixed all the fractures when they operated. The breaks were bad enough that you needed pins, plates and screws, which is why you've got the metal external fixators on both of them, and you'll need at least one more surgery. But so far you're not going to lose your legs."

That should have made him sag in relief but he could tell from her tormented expression that she wasn't telling him the whole truth. He knew he wasn't numb down there from meds or whatever kind of freezing they'd used during the surgery. "I can't feel them. I can't *move* them. What did they *say*?" His heart was in his throat, choking him.

Rather than answer, Zahra leaned in to press her forehead to his, cupping a hand around the back of his neck as she spoke. "Shhh. They don't know yet. It's too early."

Fear snaked through his gut, cold and stark. He went rigid in her embrace, realized he was holding his breath even as his brain screamed in denial.

Paralyzed. He was fucking *paralyzed*.

"Sean, please," Zahra whispered, her voice ragged with unshed tears. "Please lie down and try your hardest to stay calm. I'm right here and I'm not going anywhere, so please…"

It was the anguish in her tone that reached him through the fog of panic and terror. And though he wanted more than anything to jump out of that bed and prove this was just a fucking awful nightmare, he couldn't move from the waist down. Nothing, not even his toes, no matter how hard he tried. His horrified gaze landed on the catheter bag they had him hooked up to and his stomach went into freefall.

Fucking Christ, he was supposed to go the rest of his life sitting in a goddamn chair with a tube in his dick and a colostomy bag hanging out of him to collect his shit? No walking or running, or even standing. His dick probably wouldn't work either. Horror and denial swamped him. He started to shake—his upper body, anyway—tremors he had no hope in hell of controlling.

"Sean, shhh," Zahra pleaded, wrapping her arms around his shoulders and burying her face in his shoulder as his head fell back onto the pillow. He could feel and hear her distress but the numbness was creeping in, his system's defense against the stark realization that this could be his new reality. And he didn't think he could take it.

"I told you, it's too early to know what will happen," she continued. "I know you're scared and I am too, but we have to give it time and let your body heal, okay? They've got you on massive doses of corticosteroids right now to help with the inflammation. When the swelling in your spine goes down we'll know more."

Sean glanced down at the IV tube plugged into the back of his right wrist, followed it up to the bag hanging from the pole. They were pumping him full of methylprednisolone, among other things. He looked away. It took everything he had to calm down enough to uncurl his fists and force a series of slow, deep breaths in and out of his frozen lungs. He kept thinking that any second now he'd wake up from this hellish dream and everything would be fine again.

Zahra raised her head to kiss his chin, his cheeks, her smile wobbling as she gazed down at him. "I love you. Hear me? We're going to take this one day at a time and get through this together, no matter what. I promise."

Shit, he was barely holding it together as it was, and that nearly broke him. Squeezing his eyes shut against the sudden tears burning there, he wrapped his arms around her slender back and held on tight, glad he could at least do this, feel her up against him. What the hell was he going to do? He was fucking terrified. "My family?" he croaked.

"They all know. Tom called them when you went into surgery and I talked to your mom when you were just out of recovery. Your parents and brother all wanted to fly over here tomorrow but I told them to hold off. I thought in light of the security situation they should wait until you're transferred back stateside."

He nodded, the motion stiff and jerky. He couldn't imagine having his family see him this way. "What about the guys?" There'd been others with him in the truck when the bomb detonated.

Zahra eased back, wiped her wet cheeks then pulled her chair up to the side of the bed before responding. "Two of the guys in your vehicle died in the blast. The other is on the fourth floor burn unit. He's expected to make it, but..."

But he may not wish he had.

Sean swallowed. He hadn't known the Feds in his truck for more than a few hours, but the news still hit him hard. Fuck. If he'd driven just a bit closer to Hunt's vehicle, if he'd pressed down on the accelerator just a bit more when they'd hit that hairpin turn, maybe the IED would've missed them. "And the others?" he forced himself to ask.

She smoothed a gentle hand over his hair. "Out hunting."

He exhaled. That was exactly the answer he'd been hoping for. "With who?" They'd be shorthanded now.

"Jordyn's acting as Blake's spotter for this one. The two of them are supposed to rendezvous with Alex and the others in another hour or so."

Sean ran a hand over his face. He remembered Blake talking to him, holding the phone to his ear so he could speak to Zahra. He'd been on the helo with Sean too. He remembered little snapshots of seeing Blake leaning over him, talking to him over the throb of the rotors and the noise of the turbine engines. "She's good. She'll do fine." And Blake would look after Jordyn well while they were out there. But fuck, it should be him out there instead of in here with his legs a dead weight in this goddamn hospital bed.

Zahra smiled sadly at him, took his hand in hers again. "We'll help from here if you're up to it tomorrow."

Fuck, he didn't know what he was going to be up for until he got the final word on his legs from the doctors. Right now it was all he could do to keep from screaming. The rage was there along with the helplessness, twining together to simmer deep in his gut. He was afraid to even hope he might be able to walk again, but he just couldn't accept that it might never happen. What if the swelling went down and he still couldn't move his legs? "How did they target us?" he demanded instead, desperate for answers.

She shook her head, more tears glistening in her eyes. "Someone alerted Hassani's network when you crossed the border yesterday. Either one of the border guards, or someone monitoring a satellite somewhere. We think whoever carried out the attack had the bomb in place at least the night before you crossed over. Claire's checking out satellite feeds and chatter right now to see if she can find any more leads. I'd have helped her but I just couldn't concentrate until you woke up and I got to see for myself that you're okay." Her voice broke and she put a hand to her mouth as she fought back more tears.

He wasn't fucking *okay*. He clenched his jaw to keep from snarling the words at her, stared down at his dead legs instead and felt that black hole of fear yawning before him again. "I want those fuckers to pay, Zahra." Most of all, he wanted Hassani dead for everything he'd done.

She squeezed his hand in silent understanding. "We're gonna get him, Sean." Her tone was low, deadly. "We're gonna get them *all*."

The simple mud brick house had armed guards posted at every exit and entrance.

Hidden in an interior room that backed right into the mountain, Malik kept his back to the wall as he surveyed the men gathered around the circle, keeping his line of sight clear. Five Taliban leaders, including the man leading the TTP cell Malik had garnered the trust of over the past few months. Not that he trusted any of them in turn.

They were all seated on carpets that the host had placed on the dirt floor, sipping cups of hot, fragrant tea as they discussed their overall strategy that Malik had outlined using maps. At one point he'd made a drawing in the dirt in the middle of the circle to ensure even the illiterate understood what to do.

"Your men performed well this morning," he said in Pashto to one of the younger leaders in the group, a short and stocky man with a heavy black beard. "The reports say two Americans were killed and two more were badly wounded." It was a promising start for this operation. The bombing had not only eliminated some of the NSA team members, it had also started the chain of events that would culminate in the coming battle. Whenever that took place.

"My men were honored to carry out the attack."

Malik inclined his head slightly. Having men like the Taliban fighters at his disposal was incredibly useful. Their willingness to die in the fight made them invaluable for what he had in mind. "The survivors will be coming once they verify my location, and we don't know yet what kind of force they'll be bringing with them."

"It does not matter," another leader said from the other side of the circle. "However many men they bring, they will all die in these hills." A chorus of agreement rose up from the group.

Malik smiled and sipped his tea. So much easier to make this succeed when he had a large number of men willing to do his dirty work for him. All he needed was for them to buy him enough of a window to escape back across the border and make it to Islamabad. If he could make it that far without being killed or captured, his allies in the military would guard him the rest of the way until the end goal was accomplished. "You all have the weapons I provided stored away?" The men all nodded. "Excellent."

The conversation flowed around the circle for a while after that until Bashir swept the heavy rug at the entrance aside and stepped into the room with the satellite phone in his hand. "Sir?"

Malik excused himself and took the phone into a different room before answering in Urdu.

"That thing you asked me about?"

He tensed as he recognized the voice of his contact within the ISI. This was it. "What about it?"

"There's movement."

A subtle warmth spread through him, almost like the tingle of anticipation. "How close?"

"About six kilometers to your southwest. Four of them. On foot."

Only four? Malik frowned. Alex Rycroft was many things, but stupid wasn't one of them. Malik had learned everything he could about the man's background from the mole he'd used—Rycroft's own personal assistant—and through his sources within the ISI. By all indications, Rycroft made for a dangerous and determined adversary. Malik expected him to act quickly and aggressively after this morning's bombing.

"No others?" That didn't make any sense at all. After the bombing, he was sure the former Green Beret would gather reinforcements from one of the other American agencies.

"None that we can see."

The aerial view from the satellite would show that fairly clearly, especially with the heat signatures it gave. "When did you last check their position?"

"Five minutes ago."

That surprised him too.

"Good luck." The man hung up.

Malik lowered the phone, still frowning. Good luck? He didn't need luck, not with only four men coming after him. Even when Rycroft's team traced the call to this location, the

Taliban fighters could easily eliminate them all. No, there had to be more to this. He'd be very disappointed if Rycroft didn't have at least a team of Rangers or SEALs to come after him as well.

Trying to guess what his adversary's next move would be, Malik made his way back into the cramped back room. The leaders all looked up at him expectantly as he took his seat against the wall again. "The Americans have just been spotted on satellite a few kilometers away from here. So far there are only four of them."

The eldest leader, a white-bearded man likely somewhere in his late sixties, scoffed at the news. "My men can take them all in one attack. They brought no one else here?"

"Not yet." But there had to be a reason. And killing even those four wouldn't be as easy as this elder believed. Not with their experience and elite military backgrounds. He glanced around the circle. "You all understand what to do, and what is expected of you and your men?" Nods all around. "Very good."

One man held up his cup. "Death to the infidels!" The others chorused in agreement.

Malik reclined onto his hip and elbow as he raised his cup in salute to that sentiment. The time had come for a strong leader to take the reins of power in Pakistan. His country would no longer kowtow to America's every whim. "Enjoy your tea, then I want you to take up the positions we discussed." He expected that the NSA would have locked onto the satellite phone's transmission and perhaps even broken the encryption to decipher the conversation within the next hour.

Malik smiled into his cup. So far everything was going exactly as he'd planned.

CHAPTER TWELVE

I n light of them being short on manpower and dealing with time sensitive and perishable intel, Jordyn knew it made sense for her to be tapped as Blake's spotter. Still, she couldn't quite stem the nerves humming inside her as she and Blake rode the motorbikes she'd quickly finished repairing a few hours ago.

After crossing the border, they'd driven the same stretch of the Khyber Pass where the IED had taken out Dunphy's vehicle. It had made her skin crawl to see the remnants of the blackened bits of metal scattered at the side of the road. Pausing only to cammy up their faces and hands, they were now headed to the rendezvous point Alex had established here in the Spin Ghar Mountains. The others had already been broken into two-man teams, but both Lang and Wright had to stay back at the TOC to guard Claire, along with the sensitive information and equipment housed there.

Overhead the sky was a moonless veil of black above them, punctuated by millions of stars. Her night vision goggles allowed her to follow the harsh terrain without losing Blake or crashing the bike in a ravine. She opened the throttle to follow him up through a shallow wadi, the dry hard-packed dirt spraying a bit beneath her tires as she reached the crest of it and hit level ground at the top. The noise was a risk in this quiet, desolate landscape, but the bikes would get her and Blake up into the hills way faster than covering the distance on foot.

Once they met up with the others and reviewed the plan of attack, they could get close to their final position on the bikes then move out on foot until they'd found a good hide to set up in for the night. As soon as they got confirmation from Claire or obtained a visual from one of the ground team members that Hassani was in that village, they would act. And act hard. Every single one of them wanted Hassani brought to justice for what he'd done to Dunphy and the Feds. For everything he'd done to the team members over the past few weeks.

They reached the crest of a low ridge in the foothills and Blake cut his engine. Jordyn followed suit while he contacted the remaining ground team members via the radio in the sudden silence. When the exact location for the rendezvous was given, she followed Blake again for another fifteen minutes or so. Finally she made out the figures emerging from the thin concealment of scrub brush in the distance, the men lit up in green by her NVGs. Alex, Gage, Hunter and Evers waited for them to pull up, rifles in hand as they maintained perimeter security against threats she and Blake might not have heard or seen while on the bikes.

Alex spoke as they climbed off the silenced bikes. "You guys made good time."

"Yeah, not bad," Blake said, putting down his kickstand. "Any news yet?"

"Claire's been trying to locate Sand Viper by tracking the Taliban leaders known to support him," Alex answered, using Hassani's code name as an added precaution in case they were overheard somehow. With Hassani being former ISI and still having help from at least one contact in the agency, it wasn't out of the realm of possibility. "Got a few hits on the men from the meeting today. Then about fifteen minutes ago, Claire got a lock on a satellite phone call late this afternoon coming from the same village. She was able to break the encryption and verify one of the voices as Sand Viper."

Jordyn's pulse leaped. This was it, the break they'd been waiting for. She was both nervous and revved at the thought of helping put that son of a bitch in cuffs. Or, if need be, help direct a bullet to his center mass.

"Any trouble at the border?" Hunter asked.

"No," Blake said. "Barely looked at our ID this time. Guard was more interested in checking out the bikes."

Ever since Lang had delivered them to the Pak side of the border, Jordyn hadn't been able to shake off the anxiety eating at her. If someone at the border or in the Pak intelligence community had leaked the team's presence this morning, then it stood to reason they now knew about her and Blake's presence as well.

She just prayed that whatever means they'd used to track the convoy earlier today hadn't been following her and Blake since they'd hopped on the bikes. Nothing like running around in enemy territory with a virtual crosshairs on your back to get the adrenaline flowing.

"How's Dunphy?" Gage asked, hands on hips in the confident yet relaxed pose of a man comfortable with his surroundings. All of the men with her now had that same assertive posture, she noted. Out here on the hunt, they were all in their element. She felt safer knowing that.

"Out of recovery and up in his room," Blake answered. "Zahra's with him. Tom said they're both doing the best they can under the circumstances."

Jordyn mentally cringed at the thought of what Sean's reaction had been when he woke up and heard the news. She just couldn't imagine how that would feel.

"I want these fucking assholes *bad*," Hunter growled, his tone and body language full of menace as he cradled his M4 and surveyed the surrounding hills.

"Then let's get hunting," Evers said as he shifted his stance, clearly restless and eager to start moving.

Alex pulled on a pair of black Nomex gloves and looked at Blake and her. "You guys clear on everything?"

"Yeah, we're good," Blake answered on their behalf, sounding totally calm and sure in the face of what they had to do.

"Jordyn, what about you?" Alex pressed. Though he couldn't see her facial expression very well even with the NVGs, she knew he was an expert at reading body language and tone. She did her best to hide her nervousness. "You good to go?"

"Yes." It came out decisive at least. She wasn't worried about doing her job properly. She'd spent enough time using a spotter scope to be damn good at locating targets and estimating range, windage and elevation. She'd also spent enough time on the range with Blake over the years to know that they worked well together, but she was glad to know that he and the others trusted and respected her skills enough to include her on such an important op.

They'd just never worked together in a combat situation where lives were at stake before.

Apparently satisfied by her answer, Alex nodded. "You got enough fuel to get you to the next observation point?"

"Should," Blake answered in his typical efficient way.

"Good." Alex unfolded a topo map and went over the routes and positions one last time. "We'll head northeast from here to our target. Once there, Evers and I'll take the southeast edge of the village. Hunter and Gage the northwest, and you two," he glanced toward her and Blake, "will come around and take a position due south. Report in if you see anything."

He tucked the refolded map into one of the many pockets in the webbing of his body armor. "All we need is one clear piece of intel putting Sand Viper there. We get in close enough to verify while Blake and Jordyn provide surveillance and overwatch. Radio silence from here on out, use your call signs only. Once we locate Sand Viper, I call in the big guns. Understood?"

Big guns. The Black Ops team he had on standby for this operation. Everyone answered in the affirmative.

"Any questions?" When no one said anything, Alex nodded decisively. "All right, let's move out."

The others melted back into the concealment of the brush as she and Blake started up their bikes and headed out. The night air held a chilly bite. The flow of cold air over her as they rode made her grateful for the gloves and all the layers she had on.

They rode for another forty minutes to circle the valley and come in on the southern slope. The rugged terrain slowed their progress before Blake finally stopped again near a cluster of bushes beneath the brow of a hill. "We'll hide them here," he told her, his voice a whisper that barely carried to her in the crisp mountain air.

When they'd concealed the bikes, she felt even more exposed as she hefted her ruck and set out on foot after Blake. With the weight of her spotter scope and additional sniper rifle in there on top of her other supplies, her shoulders and back were aching within twenty minutes.

Blake carried extra water, batteries and ammo in his ruck, a far heavier load than hers, yet he moved with a stealth she'd never been able to match, no matter how much she practiced. Even though he outweighed her by a good sixty pounds of muscle, he was still much quieter on his feet. His boots barely made a sound as he trekked to the rise of the hill and dropped down on one knee to scan for danger, rifle at the ready.

She followed suit and waited for his tap on her shoulder to signal all clear before rising and trudging north. She wasn't sure how long they walked but the ache in her shoulders had become a screaming protest by the time they reached their objective for the night. It had to be close to oh-three-hundred. Heading into the witching hour, the time when enemy attention would be at its lowest.

"That looks like a good spot to stop," he whispered, pointing. She followed his outstretched finger to a natural outcropping cut into the hillside. It was big enough for them both to fit beneath, and deep enough to provide cover and concealment should anyone stumble across their position. Nodding, she headed over to check it out while he stood watch.

After ensuring there were no snakes or scorpions bunking in there already, she set her rifle down and dumped off her pack, biting her lip against a groan of mingled pain and relief. Blake came in a few minutes later as she was setting up her bedroll. He set his ruck against the rough rock wall and slung his rifle across his back, then reached for her and put his warm, strong hands on her stiff shoulders.

"Make sure you drink some water," he reminded her as he squeezed and rubbed at her sore muscles, working around the straps of her tactical vest. "Take a couple pain relievers too. Been a while since you were on a ruck march, I bet. Stretch out as much as you can before you cool down too much."

She felt like rolling her eyes and saying, *Yes, Dad.* Though if Senior could see her now he'd either be curious to see how she held up, or flat-out horrified at the whole situation. Could go either way, she never knew with her dad.

"Yeah, it's been a long time," she whispered, wincing as he hit a particularly tender spot on the top of her shoulders where the straps had dug in. God, his touch felt good.

Blake stepped closer, increased the pressure of his hands. She was already keyed up on nerves and anxiety. She could feel his heat against the backs of her legs, tempting her to throw caution aside and turn around to kiss him until there was nothing left but the blinding need he created in her.

He continued to work around the vest's straps on her shoulders with firm, methodical strokes, though she knew his gaze was constantly trained outward, scanning for any hint of danger. It reminded her that they weren't just hunting—they were being hunted in turn.

Having spent her two tours here in the Corps within the relatively safe confines of a fortified base in Kandahar, this was a brand new and somewhat unsettling experience for her. Whatever happened, she wouldn't let Blake or the others down. The thought of failing them in any way scared her almost as much as losing another of their team members.

"What about you?" she asked, struggling to ignore how his touch sparked the banked embers that glowed deep in her belly. Her nipples tightened against her bra, which was annoying and ridiculous and very uncomfortable with her vest on. There wouldn't be a repeat of what had happened in that loadout room any time soon, no matter how much she wished otherwise. Out here they had to be on constant alert and watch out for each other. Getting distracted could get them both killed. But the man was damn tempting.

"I'm fine," he answered, then surprised her by stopping the rubdown to wrap his arms around her waist from behind. He slipped his hands beneath the front of her vest. Her stomach muscles contracted beneath those thick forearms, banded like warm steel across her midsection. "Are you?" He whispered it against the nape of her neck, stirring the sensitive nerves there.

She made herself nod, desperately trying not to notice the heavy throb in her breasts and between her legs. She couldn't believe her body would still react to him this way under these circumstances. "I'll be fine. I won't let you down."

His arms tightened more, bringing her flush up against his front. She could feel the pressure of him, a wall of solid muscle behind her, a bulwark of safety and security between her and the rest of the world. Best of all, he loved her. "I know you won't. We're a good team. Never thought we'd be out here together, but I'm glad you're gonna act as my spotter."

He was? She twisted her head around to see him in the near darkness. With her NVGs pushed up on her helmet mount, she could only make out the shape of his face. "Really?"

"Yeah, really. And you know I'll look out for you."

She nodded. "I'm glad I'm with you too. You make me feel safe." Safer than any of the other team members would have. Blake's calm, confident nature had always drawn her.

A soft growl answered her. He pressed his lips to the back of her neck in a possessive kiss. "Good." His tone was pure, satisfied alpha male and it made her smile. Though she knew they couldn't take things further, she was still disappointed when he released her and stepped away. "Go ahead and sleep. I'll take first watch."

Sleep? Ha! "You sure?"

"I'm sure. Get it while you can. Things could move fast from here on out. Don't know when we'll get the chance to crash like this again."

The jetlag, the stress of everything and worry about the mission should have left her exhausted but she was still too much aware of the danger around them to think she'd just be able to hit her bedroll and crash. Still, she did as Blake said, keeping her boots on and her M4 within easy reach at her head as she lay down on her bedroll, using her ruck as a pillow.

After taking some water and a couple ibuprofen tablets she stretched out on her back and closed her eyes. The faint chirp of a few insects braving the cold sounded in the vicinity. Blake had disappeared from the shelter, no doubt having chosen a concealed position along the ridge to keep watch from.

Strangely, despite her lingering anxiety and the cold night air, fatigue pulled at her. It weighed her limbs and muddled her thoughts, sucking her down into sleep's beckoning arms. Still aware on some subconscious level that Blake was standing guard and wouldn't let anything happen to her, Jordyn exhaled, let the tension go and slid headlong into oblivion.

She woke sometime later to a hand on her shoulder. Jerking up onto an elbow, she peered blearily up at Blake's shadowy face. "What's wrong?"

"We've gotta get moving," he whispered back. "Alex reported seeing Hassani's right hand man at the village a few minutes ago."

She sat up and rubbed at her eyes, feeling suddenly wide awake. Hassani had to be close then. "What time is it?"

"Almost oh-four-hundred."

At that she dropped her hands and stared up at him. "Why didn't you wake me to take over the watch?" They either had to get moving, or crawl into a hide someplace.

He shrugged. "I knew you needed the sleep. It's all good. Come on, let's move now."

She felt terrible that Blake hadn't gotten any sleep, though it didn't surprise her that he'd gone without for her sake. Even before they'd admitted their feelings for each other he'd been like that with her, watching over her and giving her extra rest when they were out on a hunting trip with her brother and father.

After packing away her stuff and grabbing a protein bar to munch on, she slung on her rifle, checked her earpiece and followed him out of the enclosure. It was still dark out but a slight lightening over the eastern horizon told her dawn was coming fast. They had to be in position and in the next hide before the sun came up to avoid enemy detection.

"Just over a klick," Blake whispered to her over his shoulder. "We'll get a visual on the village, get set up then wait for word from the others."

"Okay." She followed him as silently as she could, aware with every step that they were racing against the rising sun.

CHAPTER THIRTEEN

Lying flat on his belly, Blake leaned into the stock of his M40A3 sniper rifle and peered through the scope. He and Jordyn were concealed in a hide site far up on a hillside on the southern side of the village. With the rising sun peeking over the hills on their right, the angle of the bright light gave them a perfect view of the comings and goings down in the little valley.

So far he'd only seen two civilians out and about; a young boy and an old man who'd left one of the houses on the outskirts with a small herd of goats a while ago. The target building where the meeting was supposedly held the day before was set against the eastern hillside, affording any remaining occupants good protection and concealment. Where the exit led into that hill was another story. The house's small exterior windows were covered by rugs, reducing the visibility inside to zero. Right now they had no idea who was in there. But the moment anyone emerged from that door, Blake owned them.

"Any movement?" Jordyn whispered on his left as she peered through her high powered spotter scope. They'd divided the valley in half, him taking the eastern half and her the west.

"Not yet." A big part of him still felt responsible for her being out here. This wasn't supposed to happen—she was supposed to have been safely tucked away back at HQ. He'd been careful to hide any feelings of guilt about it last night because he didn't want her to pick up on it or second guess her presence here. She was absolutely qualified for this mission, and he knew she'd perform almost as well as Dunphy would have. Blake just had a hard time putting aside his protectiveness toward her, something he had to make happen in order to do his job and defend his teammates.

He lay very still and kept his eye to his scope. Jordyn was a total pro, exercising a helluva lot more discipline than most people possessed when forced to stay in one position for an extended period of time. Aside from the rare shift or slight fidget, she didn't move beside him.

Then Hunter's voice came through their earpieces. "Got movement two hundred yards northwest of the village. Ellis, you copy?"

"I copy," Blake responded, shifting his sights to the area Hunter had indicated. Sure enough, two men emerged from what appeared to be an opening Blake hadn't noticed before in the hillside. "I see them. Stand by." He spoke to Jordyn quietly. "My angle's not great. Can you see where they came out of?"

"No, not well." She shifted slightly to move her scope.

He said Hunter's call sign to alert him. "Negative on the view of the exit point."

"Roger. Heading down to take a closer look now."

"We'll move in closer to the village too," Alex added from his and Evers's position outside the village to the east. "Report any additional movement."

"Roger that," Blake answered. A few minutes later a puff of dust rose into the air to the west of the village. He was just about to ask Jordyn what she saw when Alex came back on comms.

"Vehicles inbound from your ten o'clock."

Sure enough, over the crest of a distant hill, three vehicles appeared, winding their way down the switchbacks toward the valley floor. "We're on it," Blake informed the others. He followed the trucks as they drove along the narrow dry stream bed that led to the village and parked. The doors of the first vehicle opened and two men stepped out. Blake tightened the focus to get a better look at the men's features.

"That's Bashir wearing the shades," Hunter said a moment later as the man disappeared into the mud-brick house.

"Hassani won't be far behind him," Alex added. "Wait for them both to step outside before you take a shot."

"Copy that." Without taking his eye from the scope, he spoke to Jordyn again. "I've got the building. You take the other vehicles. Got 'em?"

"Yeah."

No one else emerged from the other two vehicles and the windows were tinted too dark for them to get a look at the occupants. Almost ten minutes passed until they got another sighting. But not from the vehicles or the building they were watching.

"Movement on the north side of the valley," Alex said suddenly.

Blake shifted his focus there in time to see two more men appear from an opening in the rocks on the opposite side of the valley. "Whoa," he murmured.

Jordyn swung her scope around to where he was looking. "What the hell?" she whispered back.

"Got a potential situation here," Blake reported to the others. "Two more tangos just walked out of the base of the hill to the north. There's gotta be a cave complex of some kind."

He heard Alex curse. "Copy that. We're gonna have to fall back, see if we can trap them all before they scatter. You hold your position while the rest of us check it out." He ordered Gage and Hunter to close in from the north, saying he and Evers would herd from the east.

"Roger," Blake replied. Alex and Evers were close to the village now, less than a hundred fifty yards away from the north-easternmost building. Gage and Hunter were somewhere to the northwest, moving to the valley floor.

The rug covering the doorway of the target building shifted and a man emerged into the strengthening sunlight. Blake zeroed in on him, aware that Jordyn had tensed as she too saw the potential threat.

As far as he knew, she'd never shot an enemy combatant before. Right now he couldn't afford to think about how this might affect her, so he blocked that out and let himself slip deep into operational mode. They both had to be sharp to protect the other ground team members. He took lives because in doing so, he saved the lives of his teammates.

Through the scope he had a perfect view of his target. "Guy's got something in his hands," he whispered to Jordyn.

"Got him." They watched as he headed north.

"What's he holding?" Blake couldn't tell yet if he was a villager or a tango.

"An AK, looks like."

Blake contacted Alex this time. "You've got company coming at you. Single tango, armed with an AK. Over."

"Take him out," came the terse reply.

"Roger that." Blake had final say on what he shot at, but this militant was getting too close to where Alex and Evers were holding. The shot's report would alert everyone of their presence but they couldn't afford to take the chance that this guy would expose Alex and Evers. Unfortunately for him, his proximity to the ground team and the weapon he held made him a walking dead man. "Range?" he asked Jordyn, still focused on his target.

Without protest or questioning him about what was happening she used the laser range designator to get a reading. "Six-two-one yards," she answered, her voice steady and clear.

He did the calculation, using the cosine indicator clamped to the telescopic sight to adjust for the angle he was shooting down at, which made the horizontal distance to the target far less than the range estimate.

He made the adjustment and stilled, compensating for the nearly forty-five degree angle of the shot by holding low. "Elevation?"

"Twelve-point-two-four minutes of angle."

"Wind?"

"Five miles per hour, zero."

The slight wind was blowing directly at their faces. Blake adjusted the scope and leaned into the stock. He fitted his eye to the scope and dialed the focus ring until the crosshairs lined up on the man's chest. "Holding one inch below center mass."

"Roger. On scope," she answered, letting him know she had the target locked in her sights.

He was ready. Through his scope he could see the detail on the buttons holding the man's shirt closed. He took up the slack on the trigger and waited. One more ounce of pressure would fire the weapon. "On target."

She knew what came next, knew what it meant but she hesitated only a second before saying, "Fire when ready."

At the signal he breathed in, partially exhaled and waited for the moment between heartbeats to gently apply the remaining ounce of pressure to squeeze the trigger. The rifle recoiled into his shoulder and the round hit four inches below the man's throat, dropping him where he stood. He was probably dead before he hit the ground.

Jordyn's voice came through the echo of the report that rang around the hills. He wasn't worried yet that he'd given their position away, only that he'd maybe initiated a firefight. "Hit, center chest, target down," she said. He knew without checking that she was still looking through her scope, searching for another target. He hadn't thought it possible, but in that moment his respect for her increased even more. She was a strong, kickass partner and he was damn proud to have her at his side.

"Perfect windage and elevation. Bang on," he said, part of him hating that she was forced to stare at a dead man she'd just helped kill. He pulled back the bolt to eject the spent cartridge and reloaded a new round, then zeroed the scope. She didn't answer and he didn't expect her to. Shit, he hoped he hadn't just unleashed hell on all of them with that shot.

He had his eye to the scope again, watching for other possible targets when he heard Jordyn swear under her breath. At her sharp tone, without thinking he lifted his head to look over at her. "What?"

She had her scope trained to the west. "Take a look over there."

He shifted around slowly to peer through his own scope, and his heart sank when he saw all the men emerging from the surrounding hillsides. At least a dozen forming on the ridge to the west alone, close to where Hunter and Gage were supposed to be. Immediately he contacted the others and used Hunter and Gage's call signs to alert them. "Advise, you've got at least a dozen tangos coming up on your three o'clock," he finished.

"Roger that," came Hunter's terse reply.

"What do we do?" Jordyn whispered to him.

There was no way he could take them all out without giving away his and Jordyn's hide site. Any more than three shots and he risked the enemy guessing their location via triangulation. Then any asshole with a long range rifle or an RPG could take a pot shot at them. "We hold here and get ready to clear that ridge if they spot the others."

Hidden in the deceptive safety of a shallow wadi, Alex crouched next to Evers and surveyed the situation. They were close to the village now, near enough to be able to effectively engage anyone coming out of the target house. But Blake's warning made the nape of his neck tingle.

Across from them on the low ridge at the west end of the valley, the enemy slowly materialized at the crest. Hunter and Gage were already pulling back toward cover while he and Evers held their position. It still wasn't too late to move back. They might still be able to sneak back into the hills without being spotted. From there they could rendezvous at a safer location and regroup.

"Oh, shit," Evers suddenly breathed beside him.

Alex's heart kicked hard at the sheer dread in the Fed's tone. He whipped his head around to follow Evers's line of sight, and looked through his binos to the northeast. Sure enough, more men were appearing on the ridgeline. All armed with what appeared to be automatic rifles.

They were being encircled. Slowly, methodically, and Alex knew this plan had been well rehearsed. Worse, he'd not only played into their hands by approaching the village, he'd led the others into the same trap with him.

He set his jaw and forced himself to keep a clear head as the adrenaline flooded his body. He tapped his earpiece. "All units fall back. That's an order."

Hunt replied with a designated mic click that told everyone he'd received and understood.

"We've still got a good line of sight here," Blake said. Not exactly an argument, but close.

"Negative. Fall *back*," Alex ordered again. As soon as the channel was clear he contacted the ops center at Kandahar, where the Quick Reaction Force was hopefully still standing by. "We're heavily outnumbered, being encircled and are moving back. Request air support to these coordinates." He yanked out his map and rattled them off. "Enemy numbers growing, using possible cave or tunnel network to move around. HVT is still in the area. Repeat, Sand Viper is still—"

A shot cracked past him on the right. Alex cursed under his breath as he and Evers automatically hit the ground on their bellies, rifles up and ready to return fire. So much for escaping unnoticed.

Even without the binos he could see more men emerging onto the far ridge, now moving down toward them in a choreographed wave. More shots rang out in the distance to the west, followed by the higher pitched sound of M4s returning fire. Gage and Hunter had engaged the enemy.

"Roger that, Dark Force one," the man on the other end of the radio answered, using Alex's radio call sign. "Transmitting your request now. QRF alerted and ready to launch within ten minutes. ETA to your position, forty minutes."

In forty fucking minutes they'd be out of ammo and likely dead. "Copy. Out."

Just that fast, the hunters had become the prey.

Alex tightened his finger on the trigger and took aim at the closest fighter to him, already at five hundred feet and closing fast. They were all in the shit now. Their only chance was to fight their way to safety.

And pray the QRF arrived in time to clear off most of those insurgents if he wanted his team to make it out of this valley alive.

★ ★ ★

CHAPTER FOURTEEN

Malik's head lifted when he heard the faint popping noise coming through the cave entrance. From where he was standing around the first bend in the rock tunnel he could make out the sound of sporadic gunfire and knew the Taliban fighters had engaged the ground team. With his back to the wall he had a clear view of the tunnel in both directions so no one could sneak up on him. He held his pistol in a double-handed grip, ready to take down anyone who came at him through the cave entrance.

The two-way radio on his belt let out a quiet squawk. He grabbed it.

"It's started. Are you ready?" Bashir asked him, his voice slightly breathless as though he'd been running.

"Yes. I'll wait for you at the exit."

"I'll be there in a few minutes."

Malik put the radio back into its holder on his belt and waited, consciously slowing his heart rate and breathing, the way he'd been taught years ago in the Pakistani military. He'd planned for this. He knew what he had to do, and that he had only one chance to execute this perfectly. So much of it was out of his control now and he hated that. Everything hinged on the fighters occupying the ground team long enough for him to make his escape. Even if the Americans had found the cave network entrances, there was no way they'd find him. And he didn't plan on putting himself in their sights anyway.

Shuffling footsteps came down the tunnel, the glow of a flashlight becoming brighter and brighter. Bashir used the Urdu password they'd set earlier. Malik relaxed his stance, but only slightly, as his most trusted man appeared out of the darkness.

"The tunnel was empty," Bashir told him, putting away his flashlight while gripping the pistol in his other hand. "No one followed. The other leaders are all busy directing their men."

"Good. What about the drivers?"

Bashir's face tightened, his mouth pinching.

Malik's muscles tightened in reflex. "What?" he demanded.

"No word yet. They should be arriving any minute. I checked their earlier coordinates myself." He shifted, clearly agitated, and Malik knew there was more.

"Say it," he snapped. He had no patience for hesitation at this point, when his survival and everything he'd worked for hinged on executing the rest of this plan.

"There's word that the tide is changing."

A bolt of fear shot through him. He masked it, kept his expression impassive even as his heart began to slam. "What do you mean," he growled. A demand, not a question.

Bashir shook his head once. "Our source at the border contacted me. He said he heard there was a warrant put out for your arrest by both the Afghan and Pakistani governments. They're planning to arrest you when you reach the border."

Malik felt the blood drain from his face. A wave of heat flooded his body, followed by a shot of ice cold fear. "When did this happen?" He watched his most trusted man carefully, studying his facial expression and body language as he awaited the answer. If he was lying or guilty of any part in this, Malik would know. He was the best there was at reading people.

Bashir didn't flinch or look away at his clipped tone, and Malik believed he was innocent of any betrayal. "Within the hour."

He frantically reviewed the possible people involved. Who had instigated this? His ISI contact? Possible, but Malik didn't have any information to go on yet. "It doesn't matter. By the time they get their forces gathered I'll already be across the border. General Sharif is sending one of his best units. They'll provide me enough protection to reach Islamabad."

"With respect, sir, I no longer think we should count on their protection."

The soft tone only made him angrier. He thrust a forefinger at Bashir. "You don't make the decisions, I do. We don't have time to argue. We have to move *now*."

Whirling away, he stormed back down the tunnel Bashir had just traveled. Crude and narrow, they still served their purpose. Over the centuries the Pashtun tribes in the area had built this vast network of tunnels interconnected by caves because of constant invasions and to evade and attack the Russians. Since the western-labeled 'War On Terror' began, the villagers and Taliban fighters had expanded them, using them as hideouts and a way to move from one location to another unseen by the American satellites and drones.

Ducking to avoid a low hanging ceiling, Malik turned right at the next bend and wound his way through the cold tunnel. This was the newest section. It stretched for nearly a full kilometer from one edge of the village to the other, beneath the mountain.

Bashir was right at his back, the soft glow of the flashlight illuminating their path. The air was cold enough here for their breath to fog. Malik moved quickly and quietly, the only sound his breathing and the faint scuff of his shoes on the dirt floor.

He'd memorized the layout of the tunnel weeks ago and could have navigated it blindfolded. A sudden left turn, then a long, winding section that traveled up toward the surface on the southwestern part of the valley. Agonizing minutes passed before finally a faint gray light seeped in from ahead. The barest echo of gunfire reached them, becoming louder with each step as they approached the exit. Just where the tunnel leveled off and bore to the left again, he paused. Bashir stopped behind him and set a hand on his shoulder, signaling he was ready to make the final run when Malik was. A silent show of solidarity and support. Malik drew strength from that.

"Check where those vehicles are," he commanded.

From his pant pocket Bashir pulled out a small device with the tracking beacon on it. He moved closer to the cave entrance to get a stronger signal. "Not far. They'll be cresting the ridge on the trail in another minute or two."

Waiting went against every instinct. It was so hard to stay put while the fight continued just beyond the cave exit and the enemy was waiting out there for him. How many and where they were positioned, he couldn't be sure. He exhaled and forced his heart rate to settle.

Finally Bashir broke the silence. "They're here. Pulling into position now."

Some of the tension released from his muscles. "Let's go." They had to time this just right. Exit too early and he'd expose himself to possible enemy fire. Exit too late, and he'd make his getaway vehicle a target.

"Let me go first," Bashir urged him. When Malik didn't stop him, he eased past to continue toward the mouth of the cave, gun in hand.

Malik followed close on his heels, alert for any hint of danger or that the cave itself might be booby trapped. When nothing suspicious caught his attention he eased his back against the rough rock wall just inside the cave's mouth and squinted while his eyes adjusted to the brightness outside. The sky was a pure, clear blue, so brilliant in the October sunshine that it blinded him for a moment. The sharp cracks of gunfire sliced through the autumn air.

Once his vision cleared he was able to see the lines of Taliban fighters closing in on the valley. He couldn't see where the ground team was positioned, but he got a general sense of their location from the direction the fighters were shooting at. As he watched, the three vehicles appeared over the rise of the hill. They picked up speed, their tires raising unavoidable clouds of dust as they sped over the dry earth.

Malik's pulse echoed in his ears. He gauged the distance from the cave entrance to where the vehicles would stop. A hundred meters, maybe less. All he had to do was sprint to the armored truck equipped with bullet resistant tires, get out of the valley and speed to the border before law enforcement could get organized there.

He counted down the seconds, his muscles tensing to make the run. He waited until the lead vehicle was close enough for him to make out the driver's silhouette through the windshield, poised and ready to break from cover and race across the open ground.

Stretched out on her stomach beside Blake, Jordyn stayed as still as possible while she surveyed the battlefield below them. To the east Alex and Evers were holding their own so far, hunkered down and leapfrogging back behind whatever cover they could find in between bursts of gunfire from the attacking Taliban. Despite the order to fall back, Blake couldn't because to the northwest, Gage and Hunter were in a far deadlier situation.

Pinned down without any concealment aside from whatever boulder they could find, they took systematically aimed shots at the insurgents swarming toward them. And they were coming fast. Over the earpiece she listened while Hunter and Gage fought their way back toward her and Blake's position.

Sighting another target taking aim at the two men, she gave Blake the range, windage and elevation. He dialed it into his scope, put his eye to it and leaned into the stock.

"On target," he said evenly, everything about him so calm and controlled despite the dire situation.

She didn't have his composure; her stomach was a concrete weight in her gut and her heart pounded.

Staring through her spotter scope at the insurgent leading the charge, she forced herself to focus on him rather than her teammates. "Fire when ready."

He pulled the trigger. An instant later the man's head snapped back, a crimson hole appearing a few inches below his throat. "Hit, upper chest," she said. The man hit the ground and didn't move but Jordyn was already locking onto the next target.

Together they methodically picked off more insurgents, and while it slowed the advance and created some confusion, it was clear the Taliban weren't giving up. Damn, what she wouldn't give for a 50 cal machine gun right now. She could clear off the entire wave coming at Hunter and Gage with one sweep.

Blake took two more shots. She heard the rhythmic click and slide of the bolt as he drew it back to eject the cartridge, then the sound of him pushing it back into place. "Ready," he told her.

She opened her mouth to give him the next target when something else caught her attention. Shifting the scope slightly to the right, she saw a line of vehicles appear over the low hill and barrel down a narrow trail that ran the length of the west side of the valley. "Trucks."

"I see them." Blake reported everything to Alex, pausing only to take another shot on his own. "Target down."

He'd dropped another insurgent who'd broken away from the line of men rushing at Gage and Hunter. She swung her scope back to the vehicles. They were slowing now, well behind where the attack on Gage and Hunter was happening. As she watched, a figure shot out from the hillside and barrelled toward the trucks. "Shit, there's another cave." Tightening the focus, she zeroed in on the man's face. Her heart seized for a second. *Oh my God.* "It's Hassani."

Blake didn't look up as he reported it to Alex and aimed his rifle at the trucks. Then, "Range," he demanded, voice holding a quietly lethal edge.

She lased the target. "Niner-eight-two." Shit, right at the extreme end of the rifle's range. Even in perfect conditions with no stress or danger of any kind it was a low percentage shot.

Alex's urgent voice came over her earpiece, the unmistakable sound of AK-47 fire in the background. "Do *not* let him get away. Stop him. *Now.*"

"Roger that." Blake settled into position. "Elevation."

She snapped out of her panic and gave him that plus the windage. "On scope. Fire when ready." Hassani was nearly to the second truck, which she was willing to bet was armored. Blake had to hit a far off, moving target or they risked losing him entirely.

He took the shot.

She held her breath as she watched through her scope. A puff of dirt rose up from the ground. Her heart sank. "Miss. About a yard left." She risked a glance at him, caught the tightening in his jaw.

The second vehicle's back door opened. Hassani was almost there. She opened her mouth to try to correct the elevation, barely caught the movement in her peripheral vision before Blake dove at her.

"Down!"

His warning shout was still registering when he rammed into her. He caught her in a flying tackle, his shoulder slamming into her ribs. A scream trapped in her throat. Everything went into slow motion. The blow sent her rolling toward the rock wall behind her. Her back slammed into the ground as Blake twisted around to absorb the impact and rolled off her.

Before she could draw a breath something plowed into the hillside below where they'd been a second before, and exploded. She jerked and instinctively dove onto her belly to cover her head. Bits of rock and earth rained down on them, pelting her back, legs and arms. The ground seemed to shake, the smell of burning cordite heavy in the air. Raising her head, her eyes widened in horror as she saw the earth beneath Blake begin to crumble. She caught the surprise and alarm on his face an instant before the ledge gave way and took him with it.

Jordyn lunged for him, swept out an arm to grab him, but it was too late. "*Blake!*" His name tore out of her, wrenched from the deepest part of her. He disappeared from view, tumbling over the edge into the valley below.

CHAPTER FIFTEEN

Jordyn's scream echoed in Blake's ears as he plunged into nothingness. He bounced off the side of the hill, slammed into a big boulder. A cry of pain tore from his throat.

He threw his hands out to grab something, anything to stop his fall, but the dirt came loose in his clawing fingers. More rocks hit him, ramming into his body with the force of a sledgehammer. He rolled and twisted, fighting to slow the slide, but it was useless.

His feet caught on something and pitched him forward, flipping him end over end in an out of control somersault. His back crashed into another rock and he tumbled down, down, until finally he hit the valley floor on his side with a bone-jarring thud.

The impact knocked the wind out of him. More rocks and debris showered him, pelting his already bruised and bloody body. Finally everything was still.

Through the ringing in his ears he could still hear the sporadic gunfire out on the battlefield ahead of him. He was exposed out here, totally helpless, the only firearm left strapped to the front of his webbing. Unsure whether his ribs or maybe his back was broken, he forced his head up. He struggled to drag in a breath.

You're not dead. Yet. Get up.

"Blake!"

Still reeling, he turned his head to the left in time to see Jordyn plunging after him. She slid and scrambled her way down the gouge he'd made in the hillside, dragging their rucks and weapons with her, completely uncaring about her own safety and that she'd exposed her position to enemy fire.

He couldn't yell to stop her, could barely get enough air to keep from passing out. Helpless, he watched her slip and bounce off a big rock before she too hit the ground with a thud, absorbing the fall with her butt.

She winced but popped up again. She ditched their gear and raced over to grab his face in her hands. Her eyes were wide and full of terror, her paint-streaked face pinched as she stared into his eyes. "Blake, say something."

"Breath," he wheezed.

She closed her eyes in relief, and released him to frantically start digging him out of the rubble he was lying in. When his lungs finally started functioning again he forced his beat-to-hell limbs to shove and kick at the debris covering his lower body, wincing every time he shifted.

"How bad are you hurt?" she demanded, running her hands over him to check for bleeding and breaks the moment he was free.

"I'm okay," he managed. He tested his legs, relieved when they moved for him, and slowly forced himself into a sitting position. They had to find cover.

She grabbed him by the shoulders, pushed him back. More pain blazed through his muscles. "Blake, no, stay still."

There were Taliban fighters coming at them and Hassani was getting away. He couldn't let that happen. "Get the rifles," he commanded, rolling painfully to his side. Cuts and scrapes stung him all over, the deep bruises all over his body already stiffening his muscles. His ribs were on fire. Hurt to fucking breathe but they couldn't afford to wait to chase Hassani down and, more importantly, they couldn't stay exposed here.

"Go," he barked. His greatest fear was Jordyn getting shot or taken captive. He'd buried it down deep but now that it was a possibility, he needed to know she was out of danger before they rejoined the fight.

She jerked slightly at the hard bite in his tone, but turned and ran back for their gear. Blake slowly got to his knees, then his feet, forcing back a groan as his battered body protested each tiny movement. By the time he was actually standing up and moving for cover behind some rocks at the base of the hill, Jordyn had the gear.

She grabbed their rucks and dragged them over to him. Biting back a groan, Blake hurried to drag them behind shelter and managed to dig out the ammo he needed while she went back for the rifles.

Jordyn was reaching for his M40A3 when he stopped her. "No, give me the fifty." It was the only weapon capable of taking out a vehicle and they hadn't needed it to this point because they'd been hunting human targets.

She met his eyes for a split second then did as he said, hauling the drag bag to him. He got on his knees to pull out the big rifle and put it together as she ran back for the smaller rifle. She was limping when she came to crouch beside him.

"What now?" she asked, hunkered down beside him, her gaze fixed on the militants still out there and closing in on them.

"Gotta get Hassani. Need to take out the truck." It was still out there. He was the only one equipped to do it at the moment, and whatever backup Alex had called in might not show up in time to do any good.

He sprawled out on his belly on the hard ground, his bruised muscles and ribs sending a searing flash of pain through him. "Gimme your earpiece," he said to her. "Lost mine in the fall." Jordyn immediately took hers out and handed it to him. As he slipped it in place she dropped beside him with the spotter scope. "Going for Hassani's vehicle," he reported to the others.

Working fast, he set up the bipod and got the Barrett M82A2 ready to fire. He set his eye to the scope and pressed the stock firmly against his throbbing shoulder. The fighters had moved back, gathering into a tighter formation south of the cave entrance Hassani had come out of. Trying to screen him. He must have already gotten into the vehicle but as Blake watched, another man was just climbing into it. The door hadn't even shut when the rear of the three vehicles hit reverse, followed by the second, then the first.

Fuck you, he told Hassani silently.

The first truck was in the way, blocking Blake from getting a clear shot on Hassani's vehicle. It had to go.

Taking aim, mentally calculating how much lead he had to give the target, he centered the crosshairs on the driver's side of the windshield and squeezed the trigger. The powerful bullpup rifle bucked against his shoulder with the recoil. Sparks of white light ignited in front of his eyes but he blinked them away and his vision cleared in time for him to see the big armor piercing round rip through the windshield.

"Hit, driver's side windshield," Jordyn reported. "Driver down." Blake was already looking for his next shot as the vehicle swerved and skidded to a halt, clearing the way for a shot on Hassani. They needed to take him alive, unless killing him was the only way to capture him. Blake couldn't shoot him now. But he could for fucking sure keep him from driving out of this valley.

The second vehicle swung in an arc to begin a three point turn.

Without pause he took aim again, this time at the engine block of the second vehicle. Not needing any help from Jordyn this time he squeezed the trigger, absorbing the kick of the recoil with gritted teeth. With grim satisfaction he watched as the big round plowed right through the engine block.

Blake smiled, the hit making all the pain he was currently in worth it. *Take that, you son of a bitch.*

Malik yelped and threw his hands up to cover his head as a heavy round slammed into the hood of the SUV, tearing through the front end. The truck shuddered and groaned. Flames burst from beneath the hood and the big vehicle came to a grinding stop.

There was no time to sit there. "Go, go!" he shouted at the driver.

"I'm trying! It won't start." Just as he said it, the fire erupted from beneath the hood in a ball of orange as the oil ignited. The man cried out and tore at his seatbelt, then frantically heaved his body up and over the seat into the back with Malik and Bashir.

Malik shoved the flailing body off him in disgust. "Get into the other vehicle," he snapped at Bashir.

Bashir reached for the door handle and yanked. It didn't open. The safety locks were engaged. The precious seconds it cost him to disable them ticked by loudly in Malik's head. Fear bubbled up inside him, stealing insidiously through his veins. They had to reach the other truck before the sniper got it.

"Go, go!" He shot a leg across the backseat to kick Bashir's door open, then shoved him out. The other man tumbled face first into the ground. Malik vaulted out, nearly stepping on Bashir's head in his haste, and frantically turned toward the remaining SUV.

The heat of the flames licked at his back. Gunfire popped behind him, where the Taliban fighters were still engaged with the American ground force. Only yards away from him, the last truck was already taking off with a spin of its tires, spewing dirt and gravel at them. Malik yelled at the driver to stop. He even pulled out his pistol and aimed it at the windshield. But the man was either too panicked to obey or a complete coward, because he reversed hard and swung the truck around in a skidding arc, then drove away from them.

Swearing under his breath, knowing the bullets in his pistol wouldn't pierce the vehicle's body or even the glass, Malik had no choice but to let it go. He dropped to a crouch to make himself a smaller target and cast a desperate look around. *The cave.*

Another loud bang. He swung his head around in time to see the sniper had put another bullet through the escaping vehicle's engine. The driver leaped out of the burning vehicle and ran in the opposite direction from Hassani.

Pushing to his feet, he grabbed Bashir's arm and ran headlong for the black mouth of it, not sparing a second thought for the driver who'd been at the wheel of the burning vehicle behind him. Halfway to the entrance, the unmistakable thump of rotors filled the air. He risked a glance over his shoulder and saw three Blackhawks zooming in low, and the outline of two huge Chinooks close behind them.

Tearing his gaze away, he put his head down and sprinted for cover. The noose was tightening. He could almost feel it cinching around his neck. "We have to get back across to the other trucks!" he yelled over the noise to Bashir, who was racing after him. "And make sure someone kills that damn sniper!" If not for that shot through the engine, he'd already be on his way out of the valley.

And then you'd be on the run from those Blackhawk and Chinook crews.

An icy tendril of fear threaded up his spine. He could hear Bashir's footsteps behind him, pounding on the hard ground, his panting breaths as he ran. He was talking on his radio as he entered the opening of the cave behind Malik, rattling off orders and issuing the command to locate and eliminate the sniper.

Head down, relying on the slight illumination from his flashlight, Malik ran as fast as the narrow and winding tunnel would allow. He had minutes at most to make it nearly a mile across to the decoy vehicles beside the village and get away before the assault teams in those Chinooks trapped him.

Shouts and the slap of running feet sounded behind them. Fighters from the Taliban warlords' forces racing into the tunnels in a desperate bid to escape the new threat. They piled into the tight space, blocking the only exit on this side of the valley.

Sealed inside the prison of his own choosing, Malik raced toward the only other escape remaining.

"He's inside," Jordyn confirmed, her dismay offset by a burst of relief that exploded inside her at the sight of those helos. Blake's answering growl of frustration told her he wasn't nearly as happy about the situation.

"Dammit, I thought I'd exposed him. That I had him *stranded.*"

Was he kidding? "You just made a nearly impossible shot and stopped the truck, forcing him out on foot. You couldn't have hit him without killing him and you know it." She knew it was the only reason he'd held off pulling the trigger when Hassani had leapt from the burning vehicle. "And we've still got him. He's not getting out of there." She indicated the valley with a sweep of her arm.

The pulse of the rotors got louder. Ahead of them the Blackhawks hovered in position in the center of the valley, the door gunners firing their machine guns in bursts to clear off the remaining fighters who hadn't reached the temporary safety of the caves. Behind them, the bulky Chinooks had dropped low into an in-ground hover as teams of men fast-roped to the ground and fanned out in a defensive perimeter. Jordyn peered through her scope. Ranger tabs on the shoulders. As well as at least another dozen heavily armed men with thick beards and customized gear.

SEALs maybe, or Delta. Either way, she was damn glad to see them.

Glad to finally be able to hand this mission over to their backup, she pushed out a breath and got onto one knee to check the battlefield one last time. No one was coming at them. For now at least, their part of the action was over. All the militants had scattered toward the various cave entrances, like ants whose nest had been exposed. Time to get her and Blake to better cover.

"Roger. We see you," Blake suddenly said. She glanced over at him, knowing he'd heard something over the earpiece. "Hunter reported in," he told her. "He and Gage are moving toward us, six hundred feet to your ten o'clock."

Jordyn aimed her scope in their direction and found them. "Got 'em." She stayed where she was, ready to help provide covering fire if necessary, but there was no one left to shoot at them as Hunter and Gage ran up. They were both breathing hard, their camouflage-painted faces streaked with sweat.

"You all right?" Hunter asked Blake. "We saw you go down when that RPG hit."

Apparently satisfied that they were safe enough for the moment, Blake finally took his eye from the scope and raised his head. "I'm fine," he said curtly.

He wasn't fine, Jordyn thought in annoyance, taking in the dozens of bloody scrapes she could see on his face and through the tears on his sleeves alone. Anyone could take one look at him and know that much. And the damage she couldn't see had to be way worse. Some of those rocks had been so big she'd had to help roll them off him. The man was just too proud and stubborn to admit how much pain he was in, though it wasn't going to help the situation if he did. She was worried he might have internal injuries.

Hunter's voice broke into her thoughts. "We've linked up with the sniper team," he said, one hand going to his earpiece. Was he talking to Alex? "Standing by." A pause. "Copy. We'll maintain defensive positions and report on any enemy movement we observe. Over." Hunter lowered the muzzle of his rifle and grinned down at Blake, his teeth a startling white against the camouflage paint. "Those shots through the engine block? *Nice.*"

Blake grunted a response as he gingerly shifted onto all fours, unable to hide a wince as he did so. "Thought I could slow him down enough for us to get him."

"Oh, you slowed him down, all right." Hunter's grin split into an evil smile. "Now they'll clean house." He nodded to the reinforcements, already scattering around the edge of the valley to locate and seal off all the cave exits.

"Come on." Gage stepped over to reach down a hand and help him up, though it was obvious Blake hated accepting the assistance. "Let's make sure we help these boys keep those holes plugged, huh? Smoke the fuckers right out of those tunnels."

Jordyn immediately stepped up to put an arm around Blake's waist. Now that the immediate threat against them was over she needed to touch him and didn't care if the others knew it. Blake glanced down at her. His gold-flecked eyes crinkled a little as he smiled. "We make a good team."

She smiled back, filled with gratitude at the compliment and that he didn't pull away from her touch. "Yeah, we do."

"Yep, damn fine job, both of you," Hunter agreed. A deadly gleam lit his amber gaze. "Now let's move. Time to catch a rat."

CHAPTER SIXTEEN

The last remaining exit was blocked.

Dozens of men dressed in tribal clothing streamed toward him from the opposite end of the tunnel, shouting and shoving at each other to get through the throng of bodies and into the section that led to the opposite side Malik had just come from. Not only were they blocking his escape, their stupidity and chaos were costing him precious seconds he didn't have. The last getaway vehicles might already be destroyed.

With an enraged snarl he shoved his way through the mob of disorganized men, using his shoulder like a battering ram. They were peasants, a blind flock of sheep he could control. He'd once been like them but he'd fought his way to the top and hadn't looked back. He couldn't respect these ignorant men who were content to live in poverty.

Men grunted and cursed him in the darkness, some punching or grabbing him. He barely felt the blows, focused solely on reaching that exit. It was close now, only fifty yards away.

His heart raced, the flood of adrenaline urging his body to move, move. He shoved harder, knocking men into each other as he forced his way through the blockage in the tunnel.

Ignorant idiots could die in here like the expendable pack of dogs they were.

A hand grabbed a fistful of his shirt and yanked him backward hard enough to rip the seams. Malik whirled to strike the arm away and came face to face with Bashir in the too-bright beam of the flashlight. The other man's eyes were wide, the fear on his face snaking through Malik. He would not desert his friend.

"Come on," Malik shouted. He whirled and battered his way through the knot of fighters standing between him and the relatively empty portion of the tunnel. Bashir clung to his shirt and didn't let go as they fought through the tangled mass of men who were supposed to have cleared off the Americans.

Finally they were through the clot of humanity. Shouts rose up behind them, full of fear and confusion. Followed by something that sounded like a small explosion.

American reinforcements, coming to clear out the tunnels. Or bury anyone inside alive.

Malik rushed onward, his pulse pounding in his ears in time with his rapid footfalls. Up ahead he could just make out the impression of light around the next bend. He snapped off his flashlight and ran, gearing up for the coming desperate sprint to the other vehicles. He'd be exposed in broad daylight, with about sixty meters of open ground to cover before he could get to the trucks.

More men ran toward him, their panicked shouts about advancing soldiers raking over his tautly stretched nerve endings. He *knew* the soldiers were coming. It was why he needed out of this damned tunnel.

One of the men tripped and fell. His comrades stumbled over his prone body and hit the ground, forming another blockage in the tunnel. Malik grabbed the first man he came to by the back of the shirt and flung him aside. Another shouted a threat and raised his rifle at him.

Malik yanked out his pistol and put a round through the man's forehead. The body fell at his feet and he kicked it aside with a growl. The others froze, backed up against the sides of the tunnel to get the hell out of his way.

Pistol up, he ran on with Bashir until the tunnel made its final bend to the right and rose toward the exit. Gunfire echoed from outside, sharp and precise. The sheer volume of fire told him everything he needed to know.

The Americans were already in position. And they were close. They might have even found the cave entrance.

Malik skidded to a stop and shrugged out of Bashir's grip. Outrage and denial seared his brain, but he couldn't refute the evidence in front of his eyes. There was nowhere else to go. The tunnels were too crowded now, he'd never get through and if he even reached another exit it would be surrounded also. The men around him might turn on him at any moment. This exit ahead was his only hope. He'd just have to risk it, plunge through the opening and bolt for the vehicles he prayed were still there.

"We can't go through there," Bashir protested in a loud whisper. The tension in his voice drew Malik's stomach even tighter. "It would be suicide!"

Dying on his terms was far preferable to rotting in prison, subjected to countless interrogations, deprivations of food and light and sleep if he didn't cooperate. After that there would be a long, drawn out legal process. When they found him guilty, he would receive the death penalty. No. He would not accept defeat here.

He raised his chin and took a defiant step forward.

"Malik, don't—"

Something clattered against the dirt floor up ahead. A metallic, rattling sound.

Grenade.

Malik barely had time to whirl away and cover his head before it exploded.

Smoke and debris swirled through the air, the concussion of the blast in the confined space making his ears throb and his head spin. He'd barely pulled in another breath before more clatters reached him. They exploded with a blinding flash of light that seemed to sear his retinas. Roaring in surprise, in fury, he covered his eyes and mouth. It was no use. The tear gas was already flooding the length of the tunnel.

He yanked his shirt up to cover his face. Too late. The chemical burned his eyes, nose and throat until he couldn't breathe, couldn't see. Blind, he lurched away from the smoke, heading back the way he'd come.

He slammed into someone crouched on the ground. Stumbled. Pitched forward in the darkness. He threw out a hand to keep from falling, gasped for air. The flashlight was long gone, but he still had his weapon. His fingers curled around the grip like talons, his index finger on the trigger.

Running footsteps sounded behind him at the cave entrance. The tread of heavy boots vibrated up through the ground.

"Malik."

He whirled at the unfamiliar voice. Blindly raised his pistol.

A shot rang out and a searing pain burst through his left hand. He screamed and dropped his weapon. The gas burned the moist edges of the wound as his blood pulsed from it. He clamped his jaw shut out of sheer force of will and crouched to frantically search for the gun. A hard weight slammed into his back. He flew forward. Smashed face down on the ground with enough force to expel the air from his already aching lungs.

Coughing, tears and snot streaming down his face, he was helpless as the soldier grabbed his arms and wrenched them behind his back. He screamed as the fiery burn in his wounded hand bit into him. The man pinned him to the ground with his weight and yanked a pair of flex cuffs around his captive wrists.

Denial and disbelief swirled like a numbing fog around him.

Captured. A prisoner.

"Verify target," the man pinning him growled.

Solid footsteps approached. A light shined into Malik's face. He squeezed his eyes shut and wrenched his head away as a deep voice rolled over him. "Affirmative. We have Sand Viper."

Sand Viper. They'd code named him after a deadly venomous snake indigenous to the area. How appropriate. A bitter laugh clogged his throat. One of them searched him, found the thumb drive suspended around his neck and removed it.

Everything else faded away. He stopped listening, didn't even bother fighting as he was unceremoniously hauled to his feet and frog marched down the remaining length of the tunnel. His eyes and nose were still streaming when they dragged him outside.

The sudden bright light pierced his eyelids. He squinted then forced his lids open to look around. Through his blurry vision he made out six hard-looking, bearded men clustered around him.

"Sir, got someone for you to see," one of them called out to a group of men standing near where the vehicles were supposed to have been. Even if he'd managed to get out of the tunnel, there would have been no escape, Malik realized bleakly.

The searing pain in his hand was making him light-headed. Someone roughly wrapped a bandage around it and squeezed hard to slow the bleeding. Malik bit back a scream. He'd rather die right here than give these bastards the satisfaction of seeing him as weak.

Anger and frustration bombarded him, nearly thick enough to choke on. A man detached himself from the group and stalked toward them.

Malik straightened and held himself rigid, unwilling to have anyone see him trapped and afraid. He wasn't afraid. He was disgusted. With both himself and the entire situation. The frustration ate at him like acid. He'd been so damn close to making it. His dream was dying, right in front of him. And there was nothing he could do about it.

The man came close, closer, until Malik's blurry vision finally made out the camouflage painted facial features. Dark, trimmed beard, short dark brown hair sprinkled with gray. And silver eyes that seemed to pierce right through him.

Alex Rycroft.

Malik held back a sneer of contempt as the man approached and halted a step or two away. The bastard wore an extremely satisfied smile as he took in Malik's humiliation. Enjoying it. A snarl of outrage built in his throat. He barely stayed the impulse to spit in the man's face.

"Well, well, Malik. I finally get to meet you in person. You and I have a lot to talk about, don't we?"

Malik glared a hole through the other man's face and remained silent as he looked beyond those broad shoulders to the group he'd been standing with. Familiar faces stared back at him. Hunter Phillips, Gage Wallace, Jake Evers, Blake Ellis and a clean-shaven man he didn't recognize.

All members of the Titanium Security team he'd been so sure he could wipe out today. All lined up before him, very much alive and savoring their victory while he stood in chains.

Standing beside the sniper, Ellis, the unfamiliar man on the far right shifted. A shaft of sunlight lit his clean-shaven features and Malik was stunned to realize he was looking at a female. "A woman?" he spat at Alex in disgust. The legendary operative had resorted to bringing a woman onto the team to replace Sean Dunphy? He sneered at the absurdity of it.

The smug smile on Rycroft's face turned hard, sharp enough to cut, and those silver eyes chilled to glacial. The icy hatred there burned him. "Yeah, how about that, a female spotter. Damn good one, too, since she's a big part of the reason you're standing there in cuffs right now."

Furious, humiliated, Malik clenched his jaw shut and moved his gaze out toward the valley where the distant bodies of fallen Taliban fighters lay baking in the intensifying sunshine.

"Get him outta here," Rycroft muttered to the men holding him.

Someone yanked a black hood over his face, blotting out all light. Bound and helpless, he had no choice but to stumble along as they dragged him to the waiting helicopter that would take him to whatever dark hole they planned to throw him into.

Jordyn had never been on an op to capture a high value target before, and she'd certainly never been around to see that kind of prisoner up close when they were detained. The SEALs or Delta operators who'd brought Hassani out of that cave had put a hood on him and she was glad. For a second she was sure those streaming, swollen eyes had locked on her with a look of pure loathing.

Standing between Blake and Gage, she watched the hardened warriors take the terrorist to the Chinook waiting out in the open valley, its huge twin rotors still turning slowly. The moment the detail cleared the buildings, the pilots powered up. The big helo's engines rose to a shrill pitch and the thump of the rotors beat against her eardrums.

Blake set an arm around her waist and squeezed. She glanced up at him and smiled. His eyes were so full of quiet pride and respect as he gazed down at her it warmed her all over.

Alex strode up to them and caught her gaze. "Hassani didn't like finding out that our female sniper team member had a part in his capture. Not at all." A pleased smile curved his mouth.

Jordyn snorted. "Not surprising, since he's a corrupt, evil, misogynistic piece of shit."

The others laughed. Blake squeezed her tighter, even though the move must have hurt him. "You're one of a kind, angel."

The obvious pride and affection in his voice made her blush. She ducked her head a little, embarrassed by the public praise. "So, are we out of here now?" she asked Alex.

Because she desperately wanted to be. She wanted to be able to relax her guard and not worry about her or one of her teammate's being shot at. And she wanted a long, hot shower to scrub off all the dust and grime and sweat. Then a bed and some privacy so she could take care of Blake the way she desperately wanted to.

So many things were still unresolved between them. She knew his disastrous relationship with Melissa had left him wary of commitment. I-love-yous aside, she needed answers about where he saw things going between them from here.

Alex nodded. "I'm going with Hassani. Evers, you're with me and the ST6 boys."

So it was the fabled SEAL Team 6. Another successful mission to add to their impressive record. Alex must've pulled some very impressive strings to have them on standby for this op.

"The rest of you hop on that Blackhawk," he said, indicating one of the two sleek birds waiting near the Chinook. He turned his gaze on Blake. "I'll meet you at the hospital."

"To see Dunphy?" Blake asked in confusion.

"That too, right after you get yourself checked out." Blake opened his mouth to argue but Alex cut him off. "Not up for debate, Ellis." He looked at her. "You're in charge. Make sure he goes and gets looked at. A few x-rays and a CT scan at the minimum."

Thank you, Alex. "Will do." She shot Blake a warning look and raised her eyebrow.

"All right, all right," he relented with a scowl. "No need to threaten me. I'll go, dammit."

Oh, there was every need. He was a stubborn-ass alpha male and she knew all too well how they operated. But she was glad it wouldn't be a fight to get his ass to the hospital.

Apparently satisfied with Blake's answer, Alex nodded and addressed the group, looking every bit the SF NCO he'd once been. "Mission accomplished, guys. Good job. See you back in Islamabad." He grinned and shifted his M4 in front of him as he turned and jogged out to meet the group heading for the Chinook, Evers right behind him.

"All right, let's get outta this dump," Hunter muttered, and motioned for the rest of them to follow him. He started out past the low houses clustered in front of them. The

Rangers were still doing their thing out there, flushing out any remaining militants from the tunnels and caves. Two stood guard by the edge of the village, nodded to them as they passed.

Hunter was in the lead, her behind him, then Blake, and Gage brought up the rear. She held her rifle in front of her, muzzle down, index finger resting on the trigger guard.

"I get dibs on first shower when we get back," Gage called from the back of the line.

"Fuck you, no you don't," Hunter shot back. "I'm team leader. I get first shower."

"What about me?" Jordyn demanded. "I'm the only female. Don't I get any kind of special consideration after roughing it out here with you guys?"

"Only if you conserve water by showering with me," Blake said behind her, too low for the others to hear.

She shot a mock glare at him over her shoulder, fighting a smile. "Yeah, I'll be happy to—right after your x-rays and CT scan come back clear."

He grinned and conceded with a nod. "Deal."

God, he really was too adorable.

"I heard that, Ellis," Hunter called back, but the amusement in his voice told her he wasn't the least bit disapproving of the flirtatious comment. Jordyn was pretty sure the guys had already figured out what was going on between her and Blake.

"Heard what?" Blake asked, all innocence.

"That lame come on you just laid on Jordyn," Gage answered wryly. "That was fuckin' sad, man."

"Yeah, Gage, we got some time. Why don't you give him a few pointers while we walk?" Hunter suggested as they trudged over the sun-baked ground. "Considering he's a sniper, that line was a huge miss."

Gage's snicker reached her. "Hey, good one—"

She caught the faintest blur of motion between the houses they were passing. A man appeared in the narrow alley, brandishing an AK. He aimed right at them. The weapon was raised to his shoulder, ready to fire.

Jordyn reacted. "Gun!"

Whirling, she dropped to one knee, aimed and fired twice, all in one motion. The report of her weapon ricocheted off the mud-brick walls. The round hit the man square in the chest. He dropped like a sack of sand and twitched once, the deadly AK now useless in his open hand.

"Jesus Christ," Blake breathed, clearly as shaken as she was.

Jordyn swallowed and kept her gaze trained on the body, though she was sure he was dead. The others were deathly quiet, all of them absorbing what had almost happened while they'd been joking around.

Before she could move, Gage stalked over with his rifle at the ready and kicked the fallen weapon out of the dead man's hands. He reached down and felt for a carotid pulse, then looked up at them. "Dead." His expression was hard, but as his light blue gaze landed on her, it softened into a grin of admiration. "Okay, you can totally have first shower."

A nervous laugh bubbled up inside her. Her heart was pounding sickeningly against her ribcage and all her muscles were still frozen. She felt queasy all of a sudden.

Blake's comforting hand settled on her shoulder for a second. He held his other out in front of her, palm up. She took it and allowed him to help her to her feet, trying to ignore how shaky her legs felt. If she hadn't seen that guy, he might have killed them all with one burst.

Pounding footsteps had them all spinning around to face another possible threat, but the voices called to them in

English. Seconds later, the two Rangers who'd been standing guard at the village entrance ran up. Hunter explained what had happened and they immediately called for backup to do another sweep of the houses.

"All right, everybody fucking watch their sixes," Hunter growled, checking around them for any remaining threats that might be lurking in the shadows. "Let's not get dead when we're two minutes from getting on the goddamn helo, huh?"

Jordyn was very much on board with that plan.

Hunter strode forward and led them through the rest of the village. Everyone was tense and on full alert as they cleared the last building and walked out into the open. Hot, bright sunshine flooded down on them. Even with some Rangers providing overwatch, none of the team members relaxed their guard until the helo was wheels up and gaining altitude, taking them soaring above the Spin Ghar Mountains and back toward Pakistan.

Blake's comforting warmth bathed her right side as he sat next to her. Blowing out a relieved breath, Jordyn leaned her head back against the interior wall and allowed her eyes to close.

★ ★ ★

CHAPTER SEVENTEEN

Hospitals gave Alex the heebie jeebies. Always had. Even back in the day when he'd been a Special Forces NCO, he'd hated going to visit one of his guys when they landed up in the hospital. Maybe because it forced him to confront his own mortality.

He knocked softly on the door and heard Zahra call out for him to come in. Pushing it open, he saw her sitting beside Dunphy. "Hey," he said, putting on a smile.

She was holding his hand, the one with the IV tube sticking out of the back of it. Dunphy looked bad. His face was pale beneath that black beard and his dark eyes were black and blue underneath from the concussion of the blast.

But it was the dullness in those eyes that worried Alex the most. A dullness that wasn't caused by drugs or whatever medication they had him on. No, this one was caused by a deep, bottomless depression. Dunphy was right there, poised on the edge of that dark pit. And if he fell in, he might never claw his way back out.

Alex still wouldn't insult the guy by trying to sugar coat the way things stood. "Any change today?"

"Nope," Dunphy answered. "Can't feel shit from the waist down. Can't even feel shit, actually." He exhaled, looked at the ceiling. "They keep coming in to turn me every hour or so, so I won't get bedsores."

Alex hid a wince and decided to try to lighten the mood. Was worth a shot. "Are the nurses good looking at least?"

The barest hint of a grin formed on Dunphy's lips. "Not nearly as good looking as this one," he said, squeezing Zahra's hand. The clear love and devotion between them was so strong Alex could actually feel it. He'd acted as her mentor for a long time now. From the first moment he'd met her after the accident that had killed her mother and left her permanently scarred, he'd seen the steely strength inside her. She'd worked her ass off for him from her first day on the job and he valued her technical knowledge and work ethic. When she'd met Dunphy, Alex had known immediately that something was different.

"She's a rare gem, that Zahra," Alex agreed. Even early on he'd seen how protective Dunphy was of her. And when things had turned deadly out in that Maryland forest, he'd had Zahra's back. Dunphy had more than earned Alex's approval as far as Zahra was concerned.

Dunphy eyed Alex's dirty BDUs and face. They'd all used baby wipes to clean up some on the flight back to Islamabad, but all of them still needed a good scrubbing with soap and the hottest water the hotel shower could give them. "You just get in?"

Alex nodded, his body still humming with pent up energy. "We got him."

Zahra's eyes widened. "Who? Hassani?"

"Yep." God it felt good to say that. The bastard had been on the CIA and NSA's most wanted list for over a year. He'd terrorized their team for weeks now. Longer than that, if you counted Hunter and his girlfriend, Khalia, who'd almost died over here in September. "About three hours ago."

Because they both had security clearance and Dunphy's expression was no longer dull but alert and interested, Alex filled them in on the operation. "He'd planned to stage a coup today. Even had a military regiment lined up and ready to escort him to Islamabad and help him seize power. His pride and that ridiculous ego were what caused his downfall." Alex had known they would, eventually. And that little thumb drive the SEALs had found on him was bound to have all kinds of useful information on it.

"Should have seen his face when he finally saw Jordyn standing with the guys," he finished proudly. "God if ever there was a Polaroid moment, that was it."

Dunphy grinned. Actually grinned wide enough that his teeth gleamed amidst that black beard. "Atta girl, Jordy."

She'd held her own out there and saved their asses in the village. "Glad I had the good foresight to bring her on board for this."

"Yeah, but you know she's not as good as I would've been, right?" Dunphy quickly asked.

Alex was glad to see the mischief gleaming in those eyes again. "If that's what you need to believe to make peace with yourself, you go right ahead," he said with a laugh. In the space of a minute, the suffocating atmosphere in the room had eased. The walls no longer seemed to be closing in on him and he could finally breathe more easily.

Someone knocked on the door. Zahra called for them to come in. It swung open and Jordyn and Blake strolled in. Well, Jordyn did. Blake's gait was somewhere between a hobble and a limp.

"Hey, how you feeling, hotshot?" Jordyn asked Dunphy, stopping at the end of the bed.

"Better than I was five minutes ago. Glad you guys got that fucker."

Blake grinned and headed around the bed to take a seat in a chair beside Zahra's. Alex noticed how stiff he was as he lowered himself into it.

"What happened to you?" Zahra asked, eyeing the dark bruises covering the exposed skin visible beneath the sleeves of his T-shirt. His arms looked beaten to shit. Alex could just imagine what the rest of him looked like.

"I might've fallen down a mountain," Blake answered. "Some asshole got lucky with an RPG and hit the side of the hill below our position."

"You get checked out?" Alex asked.

"Yeah. X-rays, CT scan, even an ultrasound. No broken bones or internal bleeding. I'm banged up, but still good to go."

"Other than the three thousand contusions all over your body, you mean," Jordyn pointed out, narrowing her eyes at him. Alex hid a smile, feeling sympathetic to the guy.

Not only was he going to be one hurting unit for the next few days at least, but on top of that Jordyn was gonna watch him closer than a mama bear guarding her cubs and it was likely gonna drive Blake batshit. There was something major going on between those two as well, but Alex didn't care as long as it didn't affect their performance. Whatever had happened in their personal relationship, they'd been discreet about it, and it certainly hadn't hindered their work in the field together.

"Uh, and he's not exactly 'good to go', no matter what he says," Jordyn continued, still glaring at Blake as she folded her arms across her chest. "He's not concussed but the bruising's pretty severe so he's on anti-inflammatories and pain meds. Which I'll probably have to force down his stubborn throat," she added with an annoyed shake of her head.

Alex snickered, earning a glower from Blake.

"Hey, can one of you convince Zahra to take a break for a bit?" Dunphy asked suddenly. "She's been stuck in here with me since I came out of recovery yesterday and won't leave. I told her I'm not going anywhere but she doesn't seem to believe me."

"Zahra, go grab something to eat," Alex said. Those green-hazel eyes flashed up to his and he could see the worry etched there. Like she was afraid something might happen to Dunphy if she left. But he could also see how exhausted and worn she was. These past few weeks had been really tough on her. "I'll stay here until you get back. Won't do him any good if you drive yourself into the ground and don't take care of yourself. Go on now," he urged with a wave of his hand when she hesitated.

Slowly, she pushed to her feet, casting an uncertain glance at Dunphy. "I'll just go for a quick bite."

Dunphy rolled his bruised, bloodshot eyes. "Go for a *long* bite, Zahr. Hell, grab a shower, sleep, whatever, but get out of here for a while. I'll still be right here when you get back, promise." He glanced meaningfully at his paralyzed legs and though Alex knew he meant it to be a light, flippant comment, it fell flat. Alex hid another wince and fought not to rub the back of his neck. Gallows humor was one thing, but Zahra wouldn't appreciate the dark jokes right now.

"Fine, I'm going," she grumbled to him. "Want anything when I come back?"

"Edible food. And I'll expect you to feed me by hand, too."

That got a grin out of her. "Well I'll be sure to peel some grapes before I come back and find a palm frond to fan you with too."

"Awesome. See you later. Now, get." He lifted his head to accept her parting kiss. The moment the door shut behind her, Dunphy exhaled and closed his eyes in utter exhaustion. "God, I thought she'd never leave."

Alex's heart went out to the guy. He was clearly trying to hold it together for Zahra's sake, and the mental effort was taking a visible toll. Alex glanced over at Jordyn and Blake. "If Ellis got medical clearance, why don't you two get outta here? You're all booked in a nice hotel for the next couple nights. A thank you perk from Uncle Sam for your part in the op that got Sand Viper."

Jordyn's eyes lit up. "A nice hotel, meaning they've got a big shower and limitless supplies of hot water?"

"Limitless water I can't promise. But it's got king size beds with clean sheets, and probably some of those fancy bottles of body wash and lotion," Alex said with a grin. "So go on, you guys get outta here too and let this guy sleep."

"I don't need to sleep," Dunphy protested.

"Yeah, you do," Alex said firmly. He gave Jordyn and Blake the hotel address, then parked his ass in the seat Zahra had occupied as the others left.

Dunphy turned his head to face him and threw him a bland look. "Really? I trade one watchdog in for a bigger one?"

"That's right," he said evenly. He set one ankle on the opposite knee and settled back, resting his clasped hands on his stomach. "You either sleep or you get to look at me until Zahra comes back."

Dunphy grunted and must have realized Alex meant it, because he elected to shut his swollen eyes. Within minutes he was asleep, his breathing slow and steady. Alex stayed next to him as he'd promised, trying not to look at Dunphy's legs and the outlines of the external fixators beneath the blankets.

The sight of them made Alex's skin crawl. Could've easily been him or any of the others lying there helpless. The spinal injury's only blessing was that he couldn't feel the damage to his legs. Those rods and pins and the set broken bones would have hurt like a bitch. But Alex knew Dunphy would rather take the pain without any meds than be faced with the possibility of being paralyzed.

Alex looked away and focused on the view out the window, letting his mind recap everything that had happened in that valley and mulling over how he was going to approach Hassani's interrogation.

When Zahra opened the door sometime later, Alex put a finger to his lips and stood. He walked out of the room and shut the door behind him before speaking.

"He's asleep?" she asked, trying to peer over his shoulder through the small window in the middle of the door.

"Zahra." He set his hands on her shoulders. Her gaze lifted to his, a little worry line forming between her eyes. He'd always been straight with her and wouldn't stop now. "I know you're trying to help him, be there for him every second, but you're wearing him out."

Hurt flashed in those pretty eyes. "What?"

Alex squeezed her shoulders gently. "He's not only coping with his injuries, he's trying to keep a brave front up so you'll worry less. That's gonna drain him and set his recovery back."

She frowned, her expression now tinged with guilt. "I never thought of that."

"It's okay. Just remember to give yourselves breaks, okay? You from him, and him from you. Stop hovering. God, we *hate* hovering. And brace yourself, because the longer this goes on, the harder it's gonna get. I've seen wounded guys get fucking nasty with their wives during recovery because they're frustrated and they've got a convenient target right there to yell at."

Her shoulders sagged. "God, I'm so not looking forward to that."

Might not happen for a bit, because she and Dunphy were so new, but Alex didn't doubt for a moment that it would happen eventually. "I know. Just promise me that no matter what he says or does, you stay strong. He loves you, I know that without a doubt, so when he does or says anything stupid, chalk it up to what's all bottled up inside him. And don't take shit from him when he gets like that, either. You're no one's punching bag, verbal or otherwise." He said it with such force, the protective male in him bristling at the thought of anyone hurting her.

She'd been through so much, and even though her epic fucktard of a father was rotting in a maximum security prison, Alex still wanted him dead for what he'd done to her. What he'd taken from her.

Zahra smiled fondly at his fierce tone. "I won't. His mother told me the same thing when I met her, by the way."

"Good. I'll bet she had her hands full with him as a kid."

"No doubt. God, that poor woman." She sighed, but that little smile was still there and he could see her resolve gathering again. That inner, unshakable strength he'd seen in her in a different hospital, when she'd been the one lying broken in a hospital bed. In time she'd learned to walk again. Dunphy might not be so lucky.

Not wanting to think about that, Alex drew her into his arms for a bear hug. "Hang in there, Zahr."

"I will."

"I'm here if you need me, okay? Day or night, just call or text me."

She nodded against his chest. "I know. Thanks."

He released her, waited for her to enter the room before he headed to the elevators. He texted Wright to let him know he was coming out, and the Brit pulled the SUV up to the entrance just as Alex stepped through the automatic doors.

"Where to?" he asked as Alex climbed into the front passenger seat and shut the door.

"Hotel," he answered. He was going to take that well-deserved shower and catch an hour or two of sleep before he went down to the detention facility and went head to head with Hassani. Would be interesting to see how many rounds they clocked today. Cracking someone like Hassani wouldn't be easy, but Alex had learned that few satisfying things in life came easily.

"How's your spotter doing?" Wright asked in his northern England accent as he turned out of the parking lot.

"No change so far. Don't know the final verdict on the spinal injury yet." He opened his e-mail on his phone to catch up with everything he'd missed since going out into the field. Over seventy messages popped up on screen. He scrolled through them, mentally sorting them and flagging them in order of priority. But when his eyes landed on one particular subject line, his heart lurched in his chest.

Grace Fallon.

Alex stared at it, understanding immediately what it meant. She'd taken back her maiden name. Had finally divorced that undeserving bastard.

You don't deserve her either.

He pushed out a slow breath. It didn't help. Pulse thudding, muscles rigid, Alex opened the message. After he'd seen that redhead at the market in Peshawar, he hadn't been able to stop thinking about Grace. He'd asked one of his people in the NSA to run her name and see what they came up with. Spotting her in Pesh had seemed impossible, but he hadn't been able to let it go.

He scanned the body of the e-mail, aware that his knuckles had turned white from clenching the phone. Christ, it was all he could do to remember to breathe.

> *...now working for the UN as a consultant...chemical weapons inspector...*
>
> *...last credit card transaction was last night in Islamabad.*

Alex stared at the screen, unblinking, made himself read the message twice so he knew he wasn't just imagining things. Shock reverberated through him.

Grace was here in Islamabad.

He lowered the phone to his lap, unable to process the avalanche of emotions. An image of her face swam before his eyes. Then it changed to her shattered expression on that terrible night four years ago when he'd lost her. That image had haunted him ever since. It still gutted him.

No.

His heart was beating so fast it slammed against his ribs with sickening force, and his chest felt so tight he feared it might burst open. He forced himself to pull in a long, shaky breath and exhale it. Then another. Hope and anxiety careened inside him, wild and volatile. He felt light-headed, so shaky he wondered if he was about to do the unthinkable and pass out. Or puke.

Wright shot him a sideways glance. "You all right, mate?"

No. "Fine." Fuck, maybe he was going to lose it. Hard, jaded Alex Rycroft, about to have a total meltdown because of a woman. All this time and finally Grace was not only free, she was right here in the same city. Had been for a while and he'd never even known. It was too much to take in.

Holding the phone tightly, Alex stared through the windshield and somehow got his breathing back under control, willed his pulse to slow down. Fate was a sick, twisted bitch, but for once, he was grateful for her unpredictability. He wasn't passing up this chance.

As soon as he finished with Hassani's initial interrogation, he was going to find Grace and do whatever it took to fix the damage he'd inflicted four years ago. Including getting on his knees and begging for the forgiveness she'd rightly refused him before.

Someone pulled the black hood off him. Malik blinked at the bright overhead light as his eyes adjusted. He held his head high, refusing to let his captors see the pain and dread he was battling as they escorted him through a sliding metal door into a cell. It appeared to be nine feet by nine feet, made of concrete, with a concrete slab holding a thin mattress and a wool blanket, and a stainless steel sink and toilet set into the far corner.

Finally someone took the cuffs off his wrists and then the steel door clanged shut behind him, locking him in his cage. "They'll come for you when it's time for your surgery," one of the guards muttered. An American, and not a Fed as he'd first assumed. The eyes boring into him were flat, cold. This man was hard, battle tested and experienced with handling high value target prisoners. CIA maybe, or NSA. One of Rycroft's?

Malik ignored him and went to sit on the thin mattress, keeping his back to the door. Dismissing the men on the other side of the bars. His message was clear enough because one of them snorted in disgust before they walked away.

Alone but watched from the hidden camera he knew was there but couldn't see, he stared down at his bandaged left hand. The pain had only marginally lessened since they'd given him some morphine at the medical center they'd taken him to. That American's bullet had ripped through the fleshy part on the outside of his hand and exited through the center of his palm. Three of the long bones were broken, the damage severe enough to warrant surgery to pin it all back together. Even then he might never regain full function of his hand again.

Forcing his gaze away from the wad of gauze wrapped around the wound, he glanced around the gray, severe cell they'd locked him in. He didn't know where he was because they'd kept the hood on him both to and from the medical facility, but he assumed somewhere in Islamabad, or close to it. As a former high ranking official within the ISI, he was intimately familiar with places like this. Satellite locations where high profile prisoners could be locked away in the deepest, darkest hole and no one on the outside would ever suspect.

Until now, he'd never been the one locked behind bars. He hated feeling like a caged animal, resented that they'd thrown him in such a place. And he still didn't know what had become of Bashir.

His mind replayed all the events that had led to this moment. All the possible people who might have betrayed him. And the Americans. He knew they were the ones behind it all. How much money had they spent to make his capture possible? They may have locked him up, but they'd made a very grave mistake.

They'd let him live.

There were people in powerful places who believed in him, people who wanted to see him at the country's helm. Even in here he wasn't as alone as the Americans would like to think. He would see to it that they'd regret not killing him when they'd had the chance.

Power and resolve swept aside the anxiety and sense of claustrophobia that had begun to creep in on him. When he found out who had betrayed him, they would die. And Alex Rycroft? Malik settled back against the concrete wall and closed his eyes.

Every man had a weakness. Even Rycroft. Malik would find it, exploit it and use it against him.

Before he killed him, he was going to crush the man's soul.

CHAPTER EIGHTEEN

Blake peeled his eyelids apart when the hotel bathroom door slid open. Jordyn walked out wearing nothing but a towel she'd tucked closed between her breasts. It covered her to mid-thigh but the thin material did little to disguise her body. His interest sharpened immediately, the heavy weight of exhaustion lifting at the prospect of seeing her naked.

Her short dark hair was still damp, her cheeks flushed from the hot shower. She flipped off the bathroom light, leaving weakening rays of dying sunlight streaming through the sheer curtains pulled across the window. Her gaze swept over his exposed body down to where the sheet lay draped across his abdomen and his swelling erection.

She crossed to him, a worried frown creasing her forehead. "How're you feeling?" The bed dipped as she sat beside him and reached down to stroke a hand over his bristled cheek.

He turned his face into her palm and kissed the center of it, breathing in the delicious clean scent of soap and vanilla. "Sore." His whole body ached, the contusions all over him making him feel like a major leaguer had beaten him with a baseball bat. After he'd showered he'd hit the bed and crashed within moments of hitting the pillow but he couldn't have slept more than half an hour.

"Yeah, I'll bet." She surveyed his chest once more, her gaze lingering on the nicks and scrapes and deep bruises blooming in various shades of blue and purple all over his skin.

Her hand trailed gently down his throat to where his HOG's Tooth lay in the center of his chest, her slender fingers toying with the bullet. That gentle touch shivered right through him, made goosebumps break out across his skin. "I've wanted to be able to do this for so long, but now that I can I'm almost scared to touch you," she said quietly.

He grabbed her hand and flattened it against his chest, the feel of it soothing something deep inside him. They hadn't talked about what came next for them—they hadn't had time. Though he wasn't all that romantic and sucked with words, he planned to show her by actions exactly what she meant to him. "Don't be." The pain didn't matter. He'd have to be dead before he'd pass up the opportunity to feel her hands on his body.

Her eyes flashed up to his, wide pools of deep, endless blue he could easily drown in. He caught the flare of female awareness there, that flash of heat she was trying to hide because she was afraid of causing him more pain. Then she looked down at where his hand pressed hers into his chest, right below where the tip of the hollow point round rested. "I can't believe nothing's broken."

Well he certainly hurt enough to make up for that, and there was only one cure he could think of. Her.

He was already hard at the thought of touching and exploring her the way he hadn't been able to their first time. Wanting to erase the worry he could see on her face, he reached up to cup her nape and brought her gaze up to his once more. "I'm okay, angel. Now come here and kiss it better."

She laughed softly at that but bent down to cradle his face with her free hand and touched her lips to his. The contact was soft and gentle, too gentle, because while it calmed him deep inside, he wanted so much more. He needed to feel her up against him and hear those soft cries as she sought her pleasure, her body closing around him and holding him there as though she never wanted to let him go.

Blake slid his other hand into her hair and pulled as he kissed her harder, loving the way her lips parted to let his tongue slide inside. She made a quiet sound in the back of her throat that he echoed as he stroked the softness of her mouth. The taste of mint and Jordyn filled him, her fresh, soapy scent wrapping around him until he felt dizzy.

Unable to wait any longer to touch her the way he needed, he released her hand on his chest to grip the front of the towel and yanked it away. She gasped into his mouth as the soft material fell away, revealing her naked body to him. She was all soft, pale skin and slender curves. *His.*

He growled into her mouth and cupped a firm, tight breast in his hand, rubbing his thumb against the hardened center. Jordyn arched her back and grabbed his hand to hold him to her, her breathing turning choppy.

His blood raced through his veins as he nipped his way down her chin and throat to the tender flesh he cradled. He'd spent far too much time wondering what color her nipples were. Last time he'd been too distracted to pay attention to the details because he'd been so focused on getting inside her as fast as possible.

Admiring those sweet candy pink centers now, he couldn't wait to taste her. He let his teeth nip the soft curve of her breast gently before closing his lips around the distended peak and sucking. Jordyn cupped the back of his head and moaned as she got to her knees facing him.

That moan shot right through him, pushed the excitement and hunger higher. His blood pulsed in his ears. God he loved her, loved knowing he could make her feel so good. And if the ache inside her was even half as painful as what he felt right now, he was the luckiest bastard alive to have her need him so much.

Her fingers stroked over his hair almost reverently. She shifted closer as he lavished attention first on one breast, then the other. Each time his lips or tongue tugged on that tight flesh she made a low sound of need that arrowed through him. His cock pulsed in silent demand against the sheet, but he ignored it. Their first time had been fast and rough. He'd wanted to mark her, brand her as his. He still wanted that now—would probably always want that—but this time he was going to make sure he loved her properly.

He let one hand drift down her ribcage, following those gorgeous lean curves to where the indentation of her waist flared into her hip. His fingers locked around her flesh, holding her in a firm grip as he released her nipple and tugged her toward him. "Come here, need to taste you," he rasped out, that primal need overriding everything else.

He almost groaned in relief and gratitude when she didn't balk or even hesitate at his command, but swung a thigh over his face to straddle his shoulders. As she braced her hands on the headboard his eyes locked on the delicate pink folds between her legs, now exposed to his gaze.

She was already wet, glistening, the rasp of her excited breaths the only sound in the room. His cock was so hard it was throbbing painfully. Holding both her hips in his hands, he guided her down and lifted his head until his lips brushed her softest flesh. Jordyn sucked in a breath and tensed beneath his hands, making a plaintive noise in the back of her throat. As if she was dying for more.

Oh, Christ *yeah.*

When he trailed his tongue across her softness and he got his first real taste of her he closed his eyes and groaned. The rich, tangy-sweet flavor of her arousal already had his head swimming and he'd barely gotten started. He lapped at her over and over, cherishing and worshipping her with his tongue. She squirmed in his hold, one hand going to his head to anchor him there.

So hot and ready for him. He slid his tongue deep inside her then caressed the length of her slit up to the swollen nub at the top where he sucked lightly.

Her fingers tightened against his head. "Oh my God, don't stop," she panted, her thighs beginning to quiver under his hands. He squeezed her hips tighter, demanding she let go of her control, and repeated the caresses with his tongue. With single-minded focus he savored her, teased her until she was whimpering and straining against his mouth with a gasped, "I'm close—want you inside me."

While part of him was loathe to stop what he was doing, he allowed her to scramble off him and struggled to get his breathing under control as she wrenched the sheet down over his thighs. His cock pulsed hot and heavy against his belly, the ache made a hundred times worse when she stared at him and licked her lips as though she couldn't wait to taste him in turn.

Before he could do more than reach up to touch her hair she gripped him in one cool fist and took the head of him into her mouth.

His whole body jolted, the incredible feel of her hot little mouth closing over him completely eclipsing the pain the movement caused. She sucked him slowly, eagerly, letting her gaze drift up to find his. The raw desire and enjoyment on her face nearly destroyed him.

He closed his eyes and fought to breathe through the pleasure blasting through him, his fingers winding into the short strands of her hair, urging her on. With each swirl of her tongue, each pull of her mouth, he died a little. God, he'd fantasized about this for so long that it was all he could do not to come at the sight of those gorgeous lips wrapped around his cock.

She worked him slowly at first, then faster, using his reaction to guide her movements. When he was shaking and sweating, when he didn't think he could take it another second without exploding, he eased her mouth away from him and stared down into her face. Her cheeks were flushed, her eyes glowing with pure hunger.

"Get up here and ride me like you mean it." His voice was a dark rasp, the hunger taking over.

Heat flared in her eyes. She sat up and crawled up to straddle his thighs, the slick, tempting place between her legs so torturously close to his aching flesh. "I'm on the shot and I'm clean. Do we still need a condom?"

"No." And fuck, the thought of sliding into her without anything between them made him shudder. He grabbed her by the hips and hoisted her up into position. He was so damn hard he didn't even need to line up his cock—the tip slid into her easily, that first gliding inch of penetration almost throwing him over the edge.

Jordyn murmured his name and shifted, bringing those beautifully curved breasts and their stiff nipples to his eye level. Automatically he lifted his head to take one sensitive point into his mouth. He curled his tongue around her and sucked, reveling in the whimper the friction caused. Planting her hands on his shoulders for better leverage, she sank down on him, taking him right to the hilt.

He panted against her breast, sweat gleaming on his face and chest. *Oh, fuck. So goddamn good.* She squeezed him so tight, her delicate muscles rippling around him in a hidden caress.

His head hit the pillow. Blake swallowed and hung on, transfixed by the expression of pure bliss on her face while she started to ride him, her swollen lips parted as she drew in shallow breaths.

Her eyes were heavy-lidded with pleasure, her cheeks flushed. Slow, tender strokes at first, gaining speed and force as she watched him and his response. His hands fisted her hips, fingers digging deep, guiding her movements as she pushed them both up that steep cliff to release.

Staring down at him, she arched her back and tipped her hips forward as she rocked. He knew she'd found the perfect angle when her breath hitched and her eyes fell closed. Then she slid a hand down to stroke the hard, rosy bud just above where they were joined and he almost lost it.

Releasing her hips, he cupped both breasts in his hands and rolled her nipples, wanting to give her all the pleasure he could. Her head fell back on a long, delicious moan, her hips rolling against him, sliding up and down his swollen cock.

Tiny, slick sounds of him moving through her wetness mingled with their panting breaths. Pure sensation speared through him, made all the more intense because he was sharing this shatteringly intimate connection with *her*. And her sounds. God, the little noises she made in the back of her throat pushed him right to the edge.

Blake gritted his teeth, part of him wanting this to go on forever. He knew she was close when her breathing turned choppy and her whimpers became mewls of raw need. *Fuck.* She was strong and erotic and gorgeous, better than his hottest fantasy. And she was almost there, just on the edge of coming.

"*Ride me*," he bit out, barely hanging on.

Jordyn licked her lips. Her hand moved faster between her legs, her hips rocking harder. He felt her body clench around him, those inner muscles squeezing tight, and he stared up at her face as the explosion hit. A wild, shattered cry tore free from her and she let it all go, totally uninhibited in her pleasure.

Blake dug his hands into her hips and drove up into her again and again, giving free rein to the voracious need gripping him. Her sigh of fulfilment reached him through the blinding haze of sensation, then her hands were cradling his face and her lips were on his.

The feel of her tongue gliding over his and knowing she could taste herself threw him over the edge. He locked one hand around the back of her head, kissed her hard and deep and exploded with a hoarse moan. She swallowed it greedily. He bucked up into her and came inside her. Waves of sensation tore through him, radiating throughout his entire body.

When they finally eased enough for him to breathe again he collapsed against the sheets and gave her a slow, thorough kiss before urging her to lie atop him. He hurt like hell all over but he didn't care because it had been worth it. She was worth *everything* to him.

Ignoring her protests about hurting him, he drew her down until she lay flush against his chest and belly, then rolled to the side where he tucked her into the sheltering curve of his body. Their hearts were still pounding and their skin was slick with perspiration. He smiled in satisfaction at the feel of her soft weight nestled against him, her body lax with pleasure.

She ran a hand over his back, skimming gently over his ribs. "So, what now?" she murmured against his chest.

He slipped a hand into her hair, trailed his fingers through it. "We sit tight until Alex sends us home. Don't think he'll need us here for more than a day or two."

Her hand stilled on his back. "And what happens when we get home?"

He knew she wasn't talking about the job this time. He eased back until he could see her eyes. "What do you want to happen?" A subtle tension took hold of him as he waited for her response. They were so new. It wasn't that he didn't trust her or her love for him. He did. But he didn't want to move too fast, even if his instinct was to ignore everything but his impulse to bind her to him.

"I asked you first," she said stubbornly.

He chuckled and kissed the little scowl on her forehead. "I guess it depends."

She blinked up at him. "On what?"

"You're in Virginia, and I'm based in Maryland right now. That's not too bad a commute." He'd make that drive every single chance he got just to see her, and he knew she'd do the same.

"So we're going to...date?" she asked, her tone hesitant, a little hurt.

"*Hell* no," he muttered, the possessive part of him taking over. He could have lost her today out on that battlefield. He was done holding back, no matter how fucking awkward he felt spilling his guts. "The way I see it, I'm yours and you're mine. I don't know what that makes us exactly, but it's not *dating*." The last word came out of him in a territorial growl. "No seeing anyone else, Jordyn. I couldn't stand it. And I don't share." Christ, the thought of another man putting his hands—and other parts—on her made him nuts.

To his surprise, a delighted smile lit her face. "What?" he demanded.

"I've never seen this territorial side of you before, that's all. Not even with Melissa."

That's because he'd never felt anything even close to this all-consuming need with Melissa.

Her fingers resumed their gentle stroking over his back, as though she was trying to heal him with her touch. "I like it." This time there was a smug edge to her voice.

Grunting a response, he leaned down to nuzzle the side of her neck and breathe her scent in. He wanted it imprinted in his mind forever. "I can't help it with you. You turn me into a total caveman."

She chuckled softly. "I like that too, to a certain extent. But try and boss me around or control me, and we're gonna have a problem."

Yeah, didn't he know it. He smiled against her skin, nibbled that sensitive spot he knew made her melt. Her appreciative sigh contented him. "I don't wanna control you. Except maybe in bed."

"Hmm, I *definitely* like that."

Him too. "Just don't wanna let you go," he murmured.

"That works for me." He heard the satisfaction in her tone, loved that she approved of being his and his alone. "So, should *I* tell my parents, or do you want to?"

He stopped kissing her, raised his head to stare down at her in the rosy glow of the fading sun's rays that streamed through the window. Facing Senior and telling him, '*Sir, I love your daughter and we've been sleeping together for about a week now*? The thought made him blanch. "That one's all yours, angel."

A mischievous smile formed on her lips. "I figured you might say that. But you know what? Something tells me it might not come as much of a surprise to them as you think."

He was pretty sure she was wrong about that, but wasn't going to say so. "I'll drive down to see you every chance I get."

"You'd better. But I'm not sure I'm ready to go back to work full time at the shop just yet. I might hang around Baltimore for a while myself."

She left it open-ended like that, the possibility of them staying together. The idea filled a place inside him he hadn't even realized was empty. Coming home to find Jordyn waiting for him every night? Eating dinner with her, sleeping beside her and making love to her every night? That was his idea of heaven. "I'd love it if you stayed with me. Sounds perfect."

She sighed again, the sound quiet and contented. Utterly satisfied. "Yeah, it does, doesn't it?" She pressed a string of kisses over his chest then laid her cheek against him. "I've wanted you for so long. Part of me still can't believe this is finally happening."

A knot of emotion clogged his chest. He hugged her close, rested his head close to hers on the pillow and closed his eyes. "I'm just sorry it took me so long to see everything straight."

He felt her smile form against his skin. "That's okay. You were more than worth the wait."

"You too, angel." She'd been his constant all these years. Devoted friend, fierce defender, sounding board and confidant. Now she'd be his lover and partner as well.

Blake was never letting her go.

★ ★ ★

CHAPTER NINETEEN

Three days later

"Pass me the gravy boat, will you?"

Jordyn reached into the cupboard to pull it out and handed it to her mother, who was at the stove giving the gravy a final stir. Quarts of it, because Blake loved to smother his roast, potatoes and popovers with it.

Her mother had gone all out for him once again, using what appeared to be every dish in the kitchen to make his favorite meal, including two different kinds of homemade pie for dessert: cherry and pecan. Her favorite was chocolate cream, but it was obvious that she wasn't the guest of honor tonight, even though *she* was the daughter and had just come home from a contract job that had landed her in combat and nearly gotten her killed.

Not that she'd tell her parents about that, because of security reasons. And because her mother would likely have a stroke.

Taking in the spread laid out on the dining room table and the counters before her, Jordyn wanted to roll her eyes. If Blake thought she was going to morph into some kind of domestic goddess now that they were back stateside, he was going to be sorely disappointed. Machines and vehicles she could work magic with. Food, not so much. Whatever DNA she'd inherited from her mother, the cooking part wasn't in there.

Her mother was still whisking the gravy, determined to beat every last lump out of it. "Mom, it's done, okay? Stop stirring and go sit down. I'll bring in the roast." Which was already carved and resting on a platter beneath a cozy tinfoil tent.

So Blake's roast wouldn't be cold when he cut into it.

Jordyn snorted and grabbed the platter to take it into the dining room where the table was already set. Her mother had even pulled out the good china and her crystal candlesticks for the occasion. Blake had always been a favorite guest, but him staying here as Jordyn's boyfriend had given him even higher status.

"Don't take the foil off yet—they're not even back and I don't want it to get cold."

She threw a pointed look at her mother over her shoulder. Dinner was always at six sharp. Everyone knew this, including Blake. Since he was currently down at the local pub with her father, if the meat was cold by the time they got back, it was their own damn fault. "You know, he'll still eat it cold. Trust me."

"Not in my house, he won't." Her mother's firm tone told her that arguing was futile.

Giving up, Jordyn shook her head and dutifully carted in all the side dishes until there was no room left on the table. "Table's full, Mom. I'll put the pies on the sideboard."

"No, I'm putting the blondies and lemon squares there."

Seriously? She'd made those too for him? Jordyn had to grin. Since she and Blake had arrived here last night, her mother had been a one-woman show fussing over Blake. He was still stiff and sore but he'd assured Jordyn the bruising looked worse than it felt now. Seeing those purple and green and yellow splotches all over his skin, her mother hadn't believed him.

She did his laundry, cooked for him, wouldn't let him touch the dishes, and even fluffed his freaking pillow at some point during the day because when she and Blake had gone to bed last night, there it was, his pillow all fluffed and the sheets turned down.

Jordyn had only agreed to stay at her parents' place for a couple days because it clearly meant so much to her mom. At first it'd been weird to crawl into bed beside Blake here in her old bedroom. It still felt forbidden, somewhat, to take him to her bed under her parents' roof. That only made the sex hotter though. Thankfully her old walnut four poster was sturdy and didn't squeak, so all they'd had to worry about was keeping their moans to a minimum.

Waking up next to him and falling asleep in his arms at night were the most precious gifts she'd ever been given and she savored every moment of both.

The back screen door squeaked open and the sound of male voices reached the kitchen.

"Perfect timing," her mother cried in delight, a huge smile on her face as she went to greet Blake with a hug.

Jordyn propped one shoulder on the doorjamb and watched him wrap his big arms around her mother, feeling a sense of completion she'd never imagined. Her mother had always loved Blake like a son, but now she was delirious about him. And the feeling was mutual, something that touched Jordyn immensely.

Neither of her parents had seemed shocked when she'd broken the news about the major change in their relationship. Her father had glowered at first, but later that night he'd been the one to casually say he'd gone to turn the heat on in

Jordyn's room so they wouldn't be too cold in there overnight. She knew they both approved of them being together.

"Smells good in here," Blake commented, his gold-hazel eyes locking on Jordyn's.

"It should. She's been cooking for two days for this," she said dryly as her father stepped over the threshold.

Her mother shot her an annoyed look and ushered everyone into the dining room. They joined hands across the table and bowed their heads to say grace, the way they always had, but this time Blake stroked his thumb softly across the back of her knuckles. A tiny caress to let her know how special she was to him. Such a simple touch shouldn't light her up inside, but it did.

In a few days they'd be going back to Baltimore together. Blake was still part of the Titanium team and she'd officially been hired to do consulting work for them. Alex, Evers, Hunter and Gage were still in Pakistan while Hassani's initial interrogations took place, which probably weren't going very well. Zahra and Dunphy were still at the hospital and there'd been no change in his status yet. Claire would be arriving in Baltimore tonight.

Given how beat up Blake was, Alex had sent him home to recharge for a few days before reporting back at NSA headquarters. Having him all to herself was an unexpected gift, and one she greatly appreciated. He was finally hers and she wasn't letting him go.

After dinner Blake helped clear the table over her mother's protests. He stood at the sink and dried all the dishes as Jordyn washed them. He helped her put everything away, comfortable and at home here, and when she was wiping the counters down he came up behind her to slide his arms around her waist.

He drew her back against the warmth of his solid frame and bent to brush a kiss against the side of her neck. She shivered and let the cloth drop, closing her eyes to better enjoy the feel of his lips and tongue on her skin.

"Come for a ride with me," he whispered, his warm breath caressing her.

She tipped her head back to look at him. "A ride?"

"Yeah. On the ATVs."

She blinked. "Now?" It was almost nine and pitch dark outside.

"Mmm, now. Come on." He tugged her until she followed him to the door. They bundled up in heavy jackets, knit caps and gloves and headed out into the cold October air. The scent of damp leaves and earth rose up as they crossed the yard to where the ATVs were parked beside the shed out back.

Blake climbed on one, threw her a grin and fired his up. Momentarily distracted by the sight of his ass framed in those snug jeans as he sat on the seat, she got hers running and followed him out past the creek to the trail that led up the mountain. A half moon shone overhead, illuminating the silver sheen of frost on the ground that made the grass and leaves sparkle like they'd been covered in fairy dust.

They rode up the mountain together, something they'd done dozens of times over the years with Jamie. A crisp, cold breeze ruffled the branches, racing across her cheeks like an icy kiss. Blake drove to the lookout point where the forest gave way to a bare cliff, and killed his engine. Jordyn pulled up beside him and did the same. In the sudden quiet she could hear the sigh of the wind and the faint hoot of an owl in the trees behind them.

"Still something, isn't it?" Blake asked as he took in the view.

It was. Below them the creek glinted in the moonlight as it rushed down the valley. Nestled in amongst the patchwork of fields and forest, the town lay nestled in the center, its twinkling lights glowing invitingly. The scene looked like something straight out of a postcard.

Blake got off his ATV and crossed over to swing a long leg over the back of her seat. An instant later his warmth settled against her back, those wonderfully strong arms coming around to envelop her. She laid her head against his shoulder with a happy sigh, enjoying the rightness of being with him in this peaceful place. They belonged together and always had, something she'd known deep inside all this time. She was grateful he finally knew it too.

"I love you," she whispered, her heart so full it ached.

His arms tightened, his lips brushing against her cheek. "Love you too." He was a man of few words, so she knew these ones didn't come lightly. It filled her with pride that he loved her enough to say them.

He shifted slightly, tugged off his gloves and set them in her lap. "Got something for you." When he eased his upper body away she turned slightly in the seat to look at him. He reached behind his neck, lifted something over his head, then held it up for her to see.

The hollow point round glinted in the moonlight.

Stunned, her gaze flew to his. "I can't take your HOG's Tooth."

"Yes you can." He slipped it over her head and adjusted the length so the tip of the bullet rested just below the notch between her collar bones.

"Blake," she protested, "you know it's bad luck. You're never supposed to take it off you—"

"Relax, angel, I don't think I'm in any danger of a sniper round getting me tonight."

She blinked. "What?" The man wasn't making any sense.

He smiled, his teeth shining white against his darker skin, and reached up to cradle the side of her face in his hand. "I talked to your dad today."

She frowned. "I know. You guys were at the pub all afternoon."

"No, Jordyn." His eyes were full of laughter. "I mean I *talked* to him." He lifted his eyebrows in a *hello-you-got-me-yet* look.

His meaning hit home. *Oh...* She didn't know what to say. Her heart was pounding and her mouth was suddenly dry. And it wasn't the cold sting of the breeze that was making her eyes tear up. "And you... What did he say?"

"That I'd better do right by you. Then he shook my hand and said he'd always hoped you and I would wind up together."

Oh, dammit, she was going to cry. Full-on harsh, ugly cry right in front of him. She could feel the pressure of the sobs sticking in her chest. She swallowed. "Blake..."

"It took me long enough to get my head out of my ass, so I'm not waiting another damn day. I know what I want, and that's you. You're it for me, Jordyn." He wrapped his fingers around hers where they clutched the HOG's Tooth tightly, and gazed deep into her eyes. "So wear this for me tonight. In the morning we'll go pick out a ring. We can figure out the details about everything else later, but tonight when I'm lying next to you in that bed, I want to see this on you and nothing else and know you're mine forever."

His impassioned words left her speechless. She could see them so clearly, lying naked in her bed together, the HOG's Tooth nestled between her bare breasts. She could picture the male satisfaction and hunger on his face as he drank in the sight of his most sacred symbol resting against her skin while he made love to her. Marking her as his.

She swallowed thickly even as she shivered in anticipation. The tears were there, so many she couldn't contain them. A few spilled down her cheeks even as she smiled and gave a watery laugh. He'd always been her dream. Now they could live it together.

She flung her arms around his neck and hugged him tight, still smiling as her tears wet his skin. "*Yes.*"

—The End—

Complete Booklist

Titanium Security Series
(romantic suspense)

Ignited

Singed

Burned

Extinguished

Bagram Special Ops Series
(military romantic suspense)

Deadly Descent

Tactical Strike

Lethal Pursuit

Suspense Series
(romantic suspense)

Out of Her League

Cover of Darkness

No Turning Back

Relentless

Absolution

Empowered Series
(paranormal romance)

Darkest Caress

Historical Romance

The Vacant Chair

Acknowledgements

Another shout out to my support team, Katie Reus and my hubby Todd. Also to Julieanne Reeves and JRT Editing, for helping me make this story shine.

About the Author

USA Today Bestselling author Kaylea Cross writes edge-of-your-seat military romantic suspense. Her work has won many awards and has been nominated for both the Daphne du Maurier and the National Readers' Choice Awards. A Registered Massage Therapist by trade, Kaylea is also an avid gardener, artist, Civil War buff, Special Ops aficionado, belly dance enthusiast and former nationally-carded softball pitcher. She lives in Vancouver, BC with her husband and sons. You can visit Kaylea at www.kayleacross.com.

CPSIA information can be obtained at www.ICGtesting.com
Printed in the USA
LVOW05s2310050514

384497LV00001B/33/P